Halo Parade

By Bill James in Foul Play Press

Bill James

Halo Parade

A Foul Play Press Book

W. W. Norton & Company
New York • London

First published as a Foul Play Press paperback 1998
First published 1991 by Foul Play Press, a division of
W. W. Norton & Company, New York

Copyright © 1987 by Bill James

Printed in the United States of America

Library of Congress Cataloging-in-Publication Data

James, Bill.
    Halo parade / Bill James
            p.   cm.
    "A Foul Play Press book."
    ISBN 0-88150-204-9 (hard cover)
    I. Title
  PR6060.A44H35   1992
823'.914—dc20   91-32392
                                                          CIP

ISBN 0-393-31831-1 pbk.

W. W. Norton & Company, Inc.
500 Fifth Avenue, New York, NY 10110
http://www.wwnorton.com

W. W. Norton & Company Ltd.
10 Coptic Street, London WC1A 1PU

1 2 3 4 5 6 7 8 9 0

1

'What age?' Iles asked.

'He has to be young, sir, for all sorts of reasons.'

'What age?'

'Oh, almost twenty-three,' Harpur told him.

Iles let his head sink forward and stared down at the desk.

Harpur said: 'But the lad's very experienced and clever. He – '

'No, keep his name to yourself, damn it,' Iles muttered, grey head still lowered. 'Don't tell me. Don't tell anyone who doesn't need to know. A boy's life is on the end of your tongue.'

'Point taken.' He knew Iles prized this phrase. Harpur had never intended giving him the name. Only he and Francis Garland had it. 'He's gone villain before and done well. He can think like them, talk like them, drool over their kids like them and get poxed by their slags like them.'

'Detective Constable Laurence Olivier.'

'He'll eject if there's even half a hint they've nosed him.'

'Nice. Tell me, Colin, have you considered his mother?'

'Don't know her.'

'I used to see them beaming and clapping on the benches at passing-out parades, convinced their glossy lads and daughters were off to bring social harmony through . . . through – what's that fucking Scarman farrago called?'

'Community policing?'

'Leading toddlers by the hand over zebra crossings. Well, we all know differently now.'

'Yes, no kid is going to hold a pig's trotter these days, sir. We've got to find other jobs for the men.'

'So we let a twenty-two-year-old pig infiltrate one of the dirtiest and most hairy – Does the lad's weighty experience include targets of this calibre, Col?'

'Well, not quite.'

'No, not quite. Harpur, if we lose this kid, I'll – '

'We can't get evidence any other way, sir. God knows we've been trying long enough. This is a man who's running a coke traffic worth what – five, ten million a year – in front of our eyes? He's killed twice, we know that, one of them a child of fourteen who happened to find out more than he should have.'

'Don't give me the arguments. I know them. They're beautiful. But we're still putting a babe in the fire.' Iles stood up and stared, disgust in his face, at the wall mirror meant for checking his uniform. 'Jesus, the years, the years.' He turned back to Harpur. 'The blessed Cedric Barton would never have countenanced such an operation, you know.'

'Barton's dead.'

'Not lost to our memories, though. No other chief constable I've worked under so sweetly combined physical grace, loyalty, human warmth and a brain that shone like potato peelings.'

2

Favard said: 'We just sits here. He got to come to us to make the delivery. He'll park in that lay-by, then walk to us. We can watch him coming. About a hundred yards and we can watch every step. It's nice. He always got the goods in a brief-case, left hand.'

'Sounds good,' Street answered.

'The same, same drill always. This drill been worked out so careful. Nothing can go wrong. Well, we knows him, so we knows what's in the case will be just right – weight, quality, he don't piss us about because we knows him and any pissing about and his head's in the mangle, and maybe his bird's who's called Celia, it's old-fashioned, but she looks a mighty screw.

Well, he got a nice percentage coming, so would he piss us about?'

'Too right.'

'This didn't come by no accident. It took some building. There's work here. This sort of thing don't come easy. This was built from bugger all by You-know-who all on his own. Look, first he got to find the people who will come in, not just Wood, this airline messenger boy, but all sorts. Customs, baggage supervisor, big ones at the top in the office, not chicken shit, Christ knows who. They all got to get their little bundle, what's called a retainer in business. This is an operation, so don't you do nothing that could mess it up, right? Just do what I say, and that's all. This been going on a long time and it's very nice.'

'I heard all this from You-know-who.'

'So, now you heard it from me, too. Some dumb pricks got to have it all said twice. You could be a dumb prick, how do I know? You looks like a dumb prick. I could be right.'

'Where does it come from?'

'What?'

'The goods, of course.'

'It comes from the man who brings it. He's going to walk to us from that lay-by. Didn't I just tell you?'

'Christ, I know, but where does he – ?'

'He's a flyer, isn't he? In a minute you'll see him in his uniform, plenty of bright stripes like a deck-chair. He's in all parts of the world.'

'Well, a flyer, yes, he would be. But where – '

'He gives us a couple of packets, maybe three. We hand him a nice wad. That's all. I don't know if it's all for him. Maybe he got people to see right. That's down to him, innit, not our worry? What we got to worry about is he's carrying the case like always and we gets the packets safe. What you want to know other things for, where it come from? It's not our job. This is him now. The Volvo. What the fuck you doing?' He grabbed Street's wrist and held it in a fierce grip.

'Going to flash the lights.'

'Who told you flash lights?'

'So he'll know it's us.'

'We don't flash no lights. I told you, this is all worked out, everything. You comes out the first time ever and you wants to flash lights. Did You-know-who say to flash lights? What do you think this is, the poxy navy? We don't want no Morse code. You flash them lights he'll make a run for it, he'll think something's wrong because it's not like always, and there won't be no nice packets to take back to You-know-who, and you could be a pair of ballocks short by morning. This boy in the flyer's uniform, he got to walk them hundred yards and his legs are shaking all the way even when everything is dead right. You flash them lights and he's – '

'All right, I got the picture.' Street tried to break Favard's hold.

'Well, get the picture sooner, dumbo. You was give the picture before we started. Who said add fancy bits?'

Street managed to pull free. 'Jesus, can you rabbit? If talking was thinking you'd win a Nobel Prize.'

'A funny man, with big ideas. All right, funny man. We'll see how funny you are one day when You-know-who gets tired of you and I got to tidy up for him. You won't be the first.' He leaned forward. 'Here he comes.'

The door of the Volvo opened and Street made out a man in flight-deck uniform and carrying a brief-case in his left hand. He had his peaked cap on and wore sun-glasses, though it was dark. For a second he stood near his car, and then started to walk hesitantly up the road towards the Toyota, the brief-case hard against his thigh, like a trip to the bank with takings. The Volvo was too far away for Street to read the registration.

'See his legs?' Favard giggled. 'Like a shot dog.' He wound down the window, then opened the glove compartment and took out ready a thick bundle of new twenties held together with rubber bands. There might be fifty, but Street did not ask. Street started memorizing the man's features as he approached. It might be unnecessary if Street saw the car number, but he could not rely on that. The drill was that this man walked back to his car after the exchange and then drove away, while they sat and waited. He might pass them, or he might three-point and go the way he had come.

Favard was right: this braided prince did look a bit bloody shaky. Why didn't he get used to it if he'd done his turn so often? What was he afraid of? Maybe getting hold of the twenties would turn out a tonic. A grand taken regularly could do fine things for the leg muscles. Jumpy lads like this shouldn't be running aircraft, though. He was about six feet tall and heavily made, around thirteen-and-a-half stone. Under the cap he might be fair headed, a neat nose, good square chin and a happy fat-boy's meaty cheeks. At job interviews he would make the panel think he was all calm, fibre and nice nature. When the day came he would not take much finding.

'He got a boat and the Volvo out of this nice little walk he takes every now and then,' Favard said. 'I heard he's saving for one of them châteaux France way, towers and fountains and shit chutes.'

The man's legs seemed to get much worse suddenly and Street thought for a moment he might fall. He stumbled badly, then flung up his free hand to get his balance again, and his head swung round so he was not looking at the Toyota any longer, but backwards over his shoulder.

'Christ, what?' Favard grunted.

Street saw a car approaching fast from behind the man, showing no lights. Their messenger boy must have heard the engine, turned to look and with his panic on a steep up had nearly lost his footing.

'What are they, these bastards?' Favard said.

The airline man was on a stretch of road between a wall and a hedge and had nowhere to go but on or back. You-know-who wasn't the only one who could plan a tidy operation. This Volvo driver decided right away he had better get back to his Volvo. He believed the advertising, and all that quality, tested steel might protect him. Or perhaps he remembered what his mummy had told him about always facing the oncoming traffic on a dangerous road and this was turning out a dangerous road. He began to run towards the speeding car, a plump-boy's sweaty waddle, the brief-case swinging about now as his arms flailed. Again he stumbled, pitching forward on those milk-

and-water legs, but still somehow kept upright, staggering the few paces between him and the lay-by.

But it was too many. The car reached him first, a Granada with three men in it, possibly four.

'Pull out. Block the road,' Favard screamed.

And Street heard another scream as the Granada hit the brief-case man. The Toyota started and he swung it across the Granada's route, driver's side towards the vehicle. If they didn't stop he would take the engine square in the right tit, not a big engine by some standards, but enough to give more than heartburn. All this was above and beyond the call of Harpur.

Favard yelled: 'He's lost the fucking case.'

The man fell back against the hedge as the car struck him and his case dropped on to the road out of sight under the Granada. He buckled and did go down this time, folded in against the bottom of the hedge silent after that first scream, his legs twisted all ways under him.

The Granada stopped and a man leapt from the back carrying a hand-gun, maybe an old Mauser. He raced back down the road to the brief-case and the Granada reversed fast after him, then stopped a second time. In a couple of seconds he was in the car again with the case and once more the Granada reversed, this time faster. So, thank Christ, he was not going to burst his way through.

'He'll turn in the lay-by,' Favard shouted. 'Get after them. Move it.'

The Granada backed in, then came roaring out and away.

'There's forty grand in that case,' Favard grieved.

Street had brought the Toyota around and was up into third and doing sixty when he braked hard and spun the wheel over. Favard jack-knifed on his belt. The airline man had somehow got himself to his feet and, just as they came opposite, fell again, this time headlong into the road, nearly under the Toyota.

'Christ, what you doing?' Favard bellowed.

'Our man – '

'I seen the bugger. Go over him, go over him. He's fucking ex. We'll lose them.'

10

But Street jumped out and pulled the poor groaning sod back into the shelter of the hedge. There didn't seem much of him left and if they had hit him there would have been nothing at all. His cap and sun-glasses had stayed in place through all of it and, except for the blood soaking his trousers and shoes, and the fact that his left hand did not seem altogether attached to his arm, he could still have looked winning at a job interview. When Street took the wheel again, Favard said: 'What I got is a Red Cross driver. You just finished yourself, you know that?'

Street let the Toyota do what it could, which was fair enough, but probably would not touch the Granada. Although the road was straight and long he could not see their car.

'Four miles and we're in town streets,' Favard said, 'so you got to get them before. No rubber burning in the town. It draws attention.'

'You want me to catch them or not?'

'Oh, big hard boy now. You just give them a farewell gift stopping like that. You're not never going to catch them.' He pulled a Lawman Magnum from a shoulder-holster and put it on his lap.

'Three of them and maybe four,' Street said.

'Maybe they're not all guns. The Mauser looked like someone just dug it out at Verdun. You carrying something?'

'You-know-who never said nothing about carrying nothing.'

'Because we had a system, you dumb prick, and nothing went wrong. This as fast as this Jap crap can do, for Chrissake?' He had a lean, straight-nosed face, with a very deep-set dark eyes, and was not at all bad looking by Dartmoor standards. Now though, he was glaring at Street and no signs of soul were on show.

'Well, something went wrong now. They ruined the system, maybe for keeps.' Ahead, street lights began to appear, but no Granada.

'Get your speed down. I told you, I don't want to get no attention. I'm carrying trouble.'

'Jesus, make up your mind. Fast or slow? A chase or a bleeding funeral?'

'You-know-who won't want no attention to us, whatever happens.'

'Not even for forty grand of powder?'

'Who said forty grand?' he snarled.

'You did, you dumb prick. You rabbit so much you don't know what's coming out.'

'Look, forget about the forty grand. You know what I mean?'

Street came down to thirty-five and they toured the town like sightseers, but the sight they wanted was not available. After half an hour they drove back towards You-know-who's place, Nightingale House, and Favard gave his mind to a few things.

In a while he said: 'Look, forget about the forty grand, OK?'

'You said that.'

'You-know-who – he won't want you to know figures like that. One thing he's pretty touchy about, it's figures. Don't say nothing in front of him about a figure like that, he could get unhappy. Maybe you think because he likes you so special he can't get unhappy with you, but he can. There've been other lads he liked special before and I seen it happen, especially about figures.'

'He might be unhappy, anyway, when we tell him.'

'Don't make it worse, that's all. All you got to know, we was just picking up a case that's all, nothing about forty grand. I could have them figures wrong, just shooting my mouth off.'

'That sounds like you.'

'So, you're going to forget it?'

'I'll tell him I thought the case had just a couple of copies of *Woman's Own* in it and a few old knitting-needles.'

'We got big trouble.'

'You got big trouble. You was corporal. Me, I'm only wheels. They gives me a Toyota, I drives it the best it will give, I can't do no better.'

'But you stopped the wheels, didn't you? You had to get out with iodine and mouth-to-mouth.'

'You're not going to talk about that to You-know-who, though, are you?'

Favard glanced up at him. 'All right, we just never had no chance, that's what we got to say.'

'Which is right.'

Favard was crouched forward, concentrating. He looked lost, like a child. There would be a mother for him somewhere in Somerset House. 'Maybe we say they had two cars, one to block us in. It was only a couple of minutes, but enough.'

'He might wear it.'

'Yes, two cars. I like it. What they had there was a bloody army and we didn't have no chance. We was playing it just like always, just like it had been worked out, and this army is suddenly coming at us out of the dark, we can't move.'

'Like Rorke's Drift.'

'We're lucky they didn't finish us, they had so many there, and all of it armed, sawn-offs, .45s, God knows what. That's the little tale, my friend. We couldn't do sod all against them numbers, it would of been like taking on the *Bismarck* – that's in the last war. Now, make sure you got it. Two cars, one a Granada, the other a Jag, some class, and both full of muscle and broadsides. We could of been blown out of the water. You got it?'

'Did we see any registrations if the Jag was so close?'

For a second that worried him. 'We're too busy trying to get round the bastard and looking out for the armament to think about regs. What are we, cops? What's the good of regs, for Chrissake? All right, You-know-who gets a friend to tickle the computer, but these are stolen cars, yes? It don't lead. We got pros against us here. These are people can organize and think, not a crew of bum kids picked up from borstal.'

'Too right.'

'Would they do a job in their own car? Would they, hell!' Favard sat back and grunted a couple of times, half content to have sorted it out. He looked very frightened, though.

'Who do you think?'

'What?'

'Who ran it – that heist?'

'You-know-who will know, for sure. We're going to be doing some visiting.'

'Christ, that stuff will be far and wide in a couple of hours, up God knows how many sniffers. We'll never get it back.'

'Who said we would? It's gone. But You-know-who will have who done it. Every one.'

'The whole army in two cars?'

'You-know-who will know who ran it and he'll have him. It got to be. This is a whole living going down the pan if not. I mean, he got a sweet career to think of. He's a professional man. You got to think of all the work and investment that have gone into this, like them pyramids.'

They turned into the long drive of Nightingale House.

'Got it now?' Favard whispered. 'Two cars. No chance. Christ, it could be all sorts in the trade – Loopy or Hector or Dandy Lorraine or the Snowman or even Elbow. But You-know-who will know.'

3

Harpur took the stairs to the fifth floor, not that there was a choice. The lifts were useless today and probably yesterday and probably tomorrow and maybe all right for half of half a day the day after. So much urine had been jetted on these landings in their fifteen years of life that the concrete was starting to float away from the reinforcing bars and only trog-speak graffiti was holding the place together. Did the thinkers who designed tower blocks live in them? No, sir. Did they come home to odours like these? They went home to the smell of money, and on their walls was no scrawl but framed certificates telling of the prizes they picked up for architecting prole batteries. It was night and Harpur could think of safer as well as sweeter places to be. A couple of kids daft on glue would be as dangerous on their filthy home ground as an SAS patrol.

At the fourth landing an old woman wearing Lord-knew-what collection of cast-offs sat wide-legged and gross on the ground among a spread of empty cider tins. She gave Harpur what wanted to be a smile and made it plain her all could be negotiated for.

'All right, ducks?' he asked, taking the next flight of stairs.

'Sodding poofter,' she said.

At flat 517 he did not knock but tried the door and found it locked. He waited a few moments until a train rumbled past nearby and then took off a shoe and cracked the glass panel with the heel. He let himself in and closed the door behind him. There were no lights and he brought out his pencil torch, but had a pause before switching on. He thought he could hear breathing, heavy and regular, from a room on his left. Still without a light he took a few steps towards the sound, moving very quietly. Putting out a hand he touched a half-opened door and now he could hear the breathing clearly. It sounded like a woman, and that troubled him. He risked the torch. He was in a kitchen, as neat and clean a place as he had ever seen, except that a girl of about nineteen, wrapped in a check table-cloth, was sleeping on her back along one of the blue Formica work surfaces, under a set of cupboards. Her shoes and clothes were neatly piled on a chair. She was thin but pleasant thin, not stick thin, and it looked as if the cloth went around her twice. Her skin was pale, too pale, and the bright yellows and reds of the cloth did nothing for her. A few hours ago she had carried out a very heavy job with eye make-up and most of it was still sticking, though not in all the right places now. Beneath this scatter of dust and grease she had real prettiness and her feet, sticking out towards the washing-machine, looked radiantly spruce. Harpur would not have minded taking his breakfast off any table-cloth she had been wrapped in.

There would not be much point in trying to wake her. This was a blotto sleep, an assisted sleep, and the pallor had been assisted, too. How long before she rotted the foundations of that cheery little nose through snorting? He moved the flashlight round, looking for her handbag and signs of a coke party, but found only bottles of Sinkfresh and Glassgleam.

Carefully he unwrapped the girl. She had a brief spasm of trembling and her eyes flickered, but she did not wake up. Yes, perhaps she was too thin but that could easily be put right. Above her small left breast was tattooed a jaguar, leaping towards her other breast. He still found no handbag but she was holding a man's small leather wallet. Opening her fingers he took it and went quickly through the contents. There were three fifty-pound notes and a couple of twenties. Did she do a bit on the game to finance her needs? Not that he would hold that against her. Under cellophane in the wallet's photograph pocket she had a grinning head-and-shoulders shot of Street. From her driving-licence he copied her name and address into his notebook and took an office address from a company security pass. Then he replaced everything, put the wallet back in her hand and re-wrapped her in the cloth.

Switching off the beam, he left the kitchen. There were other rooms to look at, and he resumed his one-step-and-a-pause progress through the flat. In a bedroom, kept as neat as the kitchen, he found Street, also sleeping, but fully dressed and lying face down on top of the bed. Although his breathing was easier than the girl's, this looked like a powder doze, too. Perhaps he was getting some gaudy dreams: very expensive dreams, too, unless the supplies came as a perk while he worked for You-know-who.

Harpur shut the bedroom door and put the electric light on. First he went through Street's pockets and then turned him on his back and began trying to bring him round, speaking his name, cracking him across the face, tugging his hair and shaking him. After about ten minutes there was a response. Street struggled to raise an arm and protect himself from the face blows. Harpur increased them in number and force. Street groaned, eyes still shut.

'Come on, you derelict fool,' Harpur snarled against his ear. 'Come on or I'll kick you awake. I'm going to tread on your dreams.'

'Christ, Mr Harpur?'

'You're lucky.'

'I am?' He tried to straighten, eyes opening, and Harpur took him by the collar and pulled him up until Street sat on the edge of the bed, feet touching the floor, his head hanging forward and down. He began to chuckle.

'Jesus, are you still gone?' Harpur flat-handed him heavily twice on the cheeks, nearly knocking him from the bed. The chuckling ended.

Street didn't raise his head. 'Read that guy in the *Sunday Times* colour mag saying a coke snort was like a thousand orgasms, sir?'

'Who believes ads in the glossies?'

Street wagged his head gently in joyful recollection. Then he said: 'What the hell are you doing here, Harpur? You'll bust my cover. It's dicey.'

'When you were getting your K-cums we were supposed to be meeting.'

Street did raise his head now. His face was wealed from the blows. 'God, yes.'

'I wait three hours while you're blacking out your mind and turning life into one long wet dream.'

'I had things ready, sir.'

'I know. I lifted your notes while you were dead there. I could have been anyone.'

Street slowly stood up and took a few steps away from the bed, hesitated, then tried several more, not too steadily. He swung his arms about like a cricketer loosening up to bowl. 'I'm registering OK now.' He sat down, very straight on a radiator, trying to look in control of himself. Slight, fresh-skinned, small-featured, he might have been even less than twenty-two. 'Once in a while I've got to use the stuff, sir. They all do. I'm part of the outfit, aren't I?'

'Do you know what you do when you're like that? Do you know what you say? You could be sniffing your way to brain damage – from a couple of pick handles.'

Still sitting upright on the radiator and looking respectfully towards Harpur he began to speak, quietly at first, but with his voice strengthening at the end. 'So, listen, do you want me to do this fucking job or not? Can we have some sense? Do you think this sort of work can be done without risk? If I start acting like a cop or a nun, where am I, for Christ's sake? What I'd like to know is have you ever handled an assignment like this, you personally, gone villain into a set-up with a cover name and identity, lived with them, fooled them? Excuse me, sir, but do you know the first thing about it? This is not like preparing duty rosters.'

'Don't shout, Ray. There's a bird asleep on the other side of the plasterboard, Melanie Jill Younger. Remember her? Your one thousand and first orgasm. The answer is No. It was generally thought I looked too much like a cop to go native.'

'Well, then – '

Harpur held up a hand. 'Fair enough. Do it your style. We want You-know-who any way we can. You're the only one who might sew it up for us.' He read the notes Street had prepared. They gave a description of an airline officer called Wood, a time, a road location where he was run down, and referred to a Granada with three, perhaps four, men in it, one armed with a Mauser. It did not look much on a sheet of Basildon Bond, only enough to see him dead ten times over if the wrong people picked it up. 'Wood's still alive,' Harpur said. 'For the Press, we're playing it simply as a hit-and-run, which was what we actually thought at first. But then we wondered why he was out of the car, and people at the airport said he'd been carrying a brief-case, which we failed to find. I sent for his bank state-ments, and he's too rich. I take it this should have been a de-livery and a well-informed team in the Granada came from nowhere and made a collection?'

Street's anger still sparked. 'If you know it all, why so fran-tic about our meeting? Why come here? It could be as good as fingering me.'

'I thought you might have something else. I need to know it all. And then, Mr Iles worries about you. He wants to be sure you're taking your cod liver oil. Well, you're obviously taking something. It wasn't all snatched, then? Still some personal supplies around?'

'If you start getting heavy with this airman, Wood – letting him see you know about the trade and what all – he's going to be on the hospital trolley phone to You-know-who right away, and he'll smell a leak, he's no mug.'

'Fear not. Mr Wood is simply a victim of mindless hooligan-ism on the road. What brief-case? What Granada?'

Somewhere in the flat a door slammed and a cistern began filling. Street stood up and went quickly from the room. In a moment, Harpur heard him and the girl talking. The tone grew unfriendly. He must be telling her to leave. Perhaps she had come to think of Street – or whatever name he had given her – as a supplier, and couldn't bear to break from him. Or perhaps it went deeper. After all, she did carry his picture. The arguing went on for a couple of minutes and then there was the sound of a struggle and the front door opened and shut. For a few seconds came loud yelling from the girl and she kicked the door a couple of times. Street returned. 'Very nice kid,' he said. 'Works for a firm that does You-know-who's interior décor. That's how I met her. She's got O levels and has read part of *The French Lieutenant's Woman*.'

'So what did Jamieson say when you lost this consignment?'

'We call him You-know-who, sir, in the trade. Well, he's a soft-hearted type, really. He slashed Paul Favard down the right cheek with a Stanley knife, but it was not too deep and well away from the eye. Reporters get worse in Brixton.'

'And you?'

'OK. You-know-who is reasonable, I told you. He personally brought a dressing for Favard afterwards and told him to put a new suit and a couple of shirts on You-know-who's account because of the blood. That's in Astley and York's, not C & A's. Anyway, Cliff Jamieson fancies me so I'm not going to get roughed up. It's been quite a help all along. Don't worry, I won't be bringing Aids back to girls at the club. It's nothing too fruity or laborious. He got the taste in the Scrubs. That's another bit of local colour I've had to adopt, isn't it, sir? There's nobody else available for him. Pity Favard is so bloody ugly, even before the knife work. Cliff bought me this, as a matter of fact. It's a kind of going steady present.' He pulled up his sleeve to reveal a Rolex watch. 'The times in that report are right to the second.'

'Does he know who did the snatch?'

'He says he does. He thinks so. You-know-who can't go down the hospital and ask Woody what he saw. He won't risk that. But he's doing his own checks, and there's a short list.'

19

'Hector, I suppose, and Snowman Vernon and Lorraine and Loopy Peterson?'

'All those and others, maybe. When he's sure who's behind it we're going to kill him.'

'Who is?'

'You-know-who, Favard and I. Those are the orders. Jamieson will do the actual slitting, or whatever. We deal with any protection the target's got or hold him down. You-know-who can't let it slide, can he? This was a beautifully polished international business, on the way to catching up with ICI, and he wanted to hand it on to his heirs, You-know-who and Sons. He hasn't always been gay, you see. Now, he's got to rebuild from nowhere, and what's the point in building if you leave enemies who can smash it all again.'

'Pretty,' Harpur said. 'It would be very pretty if we could get him for doing a rival, as well as for the trafficking. That should come out at twenty or twenty-five and with a judge's recommendation he should serve the whole bloody lot of it.'

Street began some rapid press-ups in patterns of four, three on two arms, one on one. 'I could look like an accessory.'

'Yes, we'll have to do some work on that.'

'I hope so. You know what juries think of cops, undercover or anything else.'

'Don't wear the Rolex when you get in the box. We'll look after you, even though you're sworn to another, you pretty thing. What's he going to make of those marks on your face? Sorry. Say you've got a rough dentist. And, listen, Ray, watch the driving. None of that ten-to-two stuff with the hands on the wheel, and accelerating out of bends. They might have seen the training-school handbook.'

4

'This is a friend of Mr Wood,' the hospital chief administrator told Harpur. 'Miss Celia Mars. She'd like to be present during your interview with him, and Mr Wood wishes her to be there. And I think you know that Mr Wood's solicitor will also be in attendance. In addition, the hospital will have a senior administrator in the room to monitor Mr Wood's condition. He's still far from fully well.'

'Sounds like a meeting of Nato,' Harpur said, 'but it's all right by me. Mind you, I don't know why he wants a solicitor present for a straightforward hit-and-run inquiry.' That was how Wood continued to explain the accident, and for the moment at least Harpur must pretend to believe it, for Ray Street's sake.

The chief administrator shrugged. 'Where insurance matters might be concerned people are very careful, and quite reasonably so, I'd say.'

'Simon was a bit startled to hear that an officer of your rank, Mr Harpur, was handling what you call a straightforward hit-and-run inquiry,' Celia Mars said. Her voice was surprisingly deep.

Harpur laid on the unctuousness. 'I'm extremely happy to say we tackle that kind of offence with maximum effort in this Force. A man injured or even killed in such an accident has been the victim of a serious crime just as if he had been intentionally wounded or murdered.'

Celia Mars gazed at him, seeming to look for something behind the words. She was no idiot.

'Well, quite,' the chief administrator remarked. 'One is happy to hear you say so. Now, as to Mr Wood: he can talk without much difficulty and his mind functions with remarkable clarity in one who has suffered so much. Perhaps his training to deal with potential crises in an aircraft is a help in that. Most of the injuries – very severe injuries – are in the pelvic area and below, though he also has some contusions on the face and head and one arm. There is an element of shock, still. You should take things very easily, and I must ask you to terminate your questions at once if the doctor indicates.'

'Who's the lawyer?'

'Mr Robin Hill-Williamson.'

Christ. 'Fine.'

'I have met him. A reasonable man, I'd say.'

'He's a lawyer,' Harpur replied.

'They stop you running riot?' Celia Mars asked.

'We don't run riots. We get knifed in them.'

The chief administrator took them to Wood's room. Hill-Williamson and the doctor were standing together at the side of the bed, and they greeted Harpur without a smile. Hill-Williamson appeared his customary bright, hired self. The chief administrator withdrew.

Wood lay almost flat, looking very bad, his legs under a cage. One arm was outside the bedclothes and in a bandage. On his forehead were two small sticking plasters, and part of his hair in the front had been shaved back and a cut there treated with mauve antiseptic. When Hill-Williamson made the introductions Wood did not look towards Harpur, though his eyes were open.

'Grand to see you looking so bonny,' Harpur told him. 'I gather they'll soon have you back in the air. And now that you can give us some idea of what happened we may be able to catch whoever it was caused your injuries.'

Harpur sat down, took out a notebook and prepared himself for the flow of make-believe.

'Did you see the vehicle that hit you, Simon?' he asked gently.

'It was dark.'

'Of course. But you could distinguish whether it was a car, a van or something bigger, I expect.'

Wood considered this only for a moment. 'A van.'

'Good.' Let the sod think the police had it all wrong. 'That was our own impression, but it's important we hear these things unprompted from you. We have tyre marks, and an officer a couple of miles along the road said he saw a van at around 10.10 p.m., which would be about right?'

He nodded and winced, as if even this small movement had hurt.

'I wonder if you noticed the colour of this van,' he asked. He was aware of Celia Mars watching him closely. She would be about thirty-five, with dark hair worn short and top-drawer cheek-bones, tall, very slim, green-eyed and certainly beautiful. As far as he could see, she sported no jewellery. Didn't dear Simon know how to put his hand in his pocket? Was he really squirrelling all the loot for a nest in France?

'Colour?' Wood said. 'I think white.'

Harpur smiled, as if very pleased. 'Good again. That also fits. Can you say what make? A Transit? Bigger than that?'

'I'm not well up in vans.'

'No, of course not. Any lettering or name on the side?'

Hill-Williamson said: 'The vehicle came towards him head-on, chief superintendent, as you know, and hit him. He's hardly likely to have seen its sides.'

'No, I didn't,' Wood replied. 'That I'd have remembered, I'm sure. After all, I want the bastard who did this to me caught. Celia and I haven't been able to talk much since it happened, but when we do it is mainly about that.'

'It's true,' she said softly.

'Did you see how many people were in the van? What any of them looked like?' Harpur asked.

'Regrettably no, on both counts.' Wood seemed more relaxed now and did glance towards Harpur and smiled an apology. Perhaps this interview was not turning out as formidable as he had feared.

'And you couldn't get a registration number?'

'It was all so fast, Mr Harpur.' He shook his head sadly.

'Some of these matters are distressing to the patient,' the doctor fluted. 'If it could be done without causing him to relive the incident I'd much appreciate it.'

'He was obviously doing a hell of a speed,' Harpur said. 'Crazy on that road, narrow, unlit.'

Wood gave another small, very wry smile and looked down

the bed towards the main damage. 'In a way I was lucky.'

'It's good you can think of it like that,' Harpur said. 'Damn brave.'

'I have to make the best of things,' Wood replied. 'I've got to live with it.'

Celia Mars said: 'What I still don't understand, really, Simon, is why you were out of the car.'

Good point, but Simon was not going to like it.

He spoke wearily. 'Just that I felt like some air, Celia. As I've told you. I'd been flying for seventeen hours. You get so damn stale. I often park there and walk a little way and come back.'

'Nice to have a bit of terra firma under you again, I should think,' Harpur said. 'Oh, perfectly understandable.'

'But such a road,' Celia replied.

'One has to assume a reasonable standard of care and skill in drivers, Miss Mars,' Hill-Williamson intoned. 'One really cannot allow a basic, very basic, freedom like the right to take a stroll to be inhibited by the fear that perhaps some criminally careless driver will be on the road.'

'Well said indeed,' Harpur exclaimed.

'Is there much more?' the doctor asked. 'He ought to rest.'

Harpur stood up and put his notebook away. 'I understand entirely.' He leaned over and took Wood's hand. 'I'm sure you're going to make a sensationally fast recovery. You've got the spirit. We'll start looking right away for this white van damaged on a front wing.' Not likely. 'We'll have them, and soon, don't worry. Should you recall anything more about the vehicle, or anything at all to do with the incident, do give me a bell.'

'I certainly will,' Wood said, his voice weakening but very friendly.

'Don't talk now,' the doctor instructed.

'I've total faith in you, Mr Harpur,' Wood said. 'I know you'll do everything in your power to help.'

'Thank you, I prize that.'

He was in the car-park when he heard a woman calling his name and saw that Celia Mars had followed him out.

'I don't believe it,' she told him. 'Your behaviour in there. So tame, so casual. Are you always like that? I could hardly accept you were a policeman, except when you ribbed the lawyer.'

'One tries to be considerate,' Harpur replied. 'After all, I was talking to a victim, not a suspect. Did you expect me to knock him about with a bunch of lilies?'

She was dressed in modish baggy brown cord trousers and a modish loose brown leather jacket, not modes he liked, but he could imagine her otherwise: with so many women's fashions he had to correct in that way, these days. In any case, although he could see she was very lovely, Celia Mars looked a bit too gaunt and classy for his tastes. She stared at him, as she had in Wood's room, and this time he stared back, trying to work out how much she knew about Wood and whether she understood that what he had said was lies from start to finish.

'Could you tell me this, Mr Harpur: did you find anything where he was run down?'

'Not that I know of. What kind of thing?'

'He always carried a brief-case when he went to work. As a matter of fact, I bought it for him. It seems to be missing. It wasn't in the Volvo, it's not at his place nor at the airport.'

'Have you asked him?'

'Well, no, I haven't yet. Perhaps when he's stronger.'

'What's your point, Miss Mars?'

'Oh, no point, I suppose. Only that I don't get what happened. Would a hit-and-run driver stop to pick up a brief-case? Why? He had money on him and credit cards. He didn't take those.'

'Most hit-and-run drivers are so panicked they wouldn't get out for anything.'

'What I thought.'

'But he'd hardly be carrying a brief-case if he was just taking a stroll,' Harpur pointed out.

'If it had something valuable in it that he didn't want to leave in the car?'

This girl had a mind. 'What would that be?' Harpur asked. 'Are you saying that the person or people who hit him knew what he was carrying and deliberately ran him down?' He watched her carefully for any sign that she knew about the pick-up arrangement with You-know-who's man.

'I understand from the airport that they'd told you about the brief-case,' she said.

'Yes? I forget. It doesn't seem too relevant.'

'Have you seen where it happened?'

'Of course.'

'I went out there. It looked as if a vehicle had braked hard. A lot of rubber on the road. You didn't have to be Nero Wolfe to see that.'

'Who the hell's he?'

'Never mind. Did you spot the marks?'

'Yes, I spotted them. That ties with a hit-and-run, doesn't it? He obviously tried to avoid Simon, then drove on scared when he failed. He would have been boozing and known he was in very big trouble.'

She lowered her head and nodded, as if half-convinced, despite herself.

'I'd be very pleased to keep you informed as we make progress. Where do I find you? At Simon Wood's address?'

'Not these days. We've been close, now and then. It's not a now period at present.'

'Oh!'

'You'll find me in the book. Mars C. G.'

'Grand.' He began to move towards his old Triumph but suddenly she put out a hand and caught him by the cuff of his jacket, then immediately released it.

'Sorry,' she said. 'But look, Mr Harpur, I've never really felt I knew Simon fully. There were parts of his life that – Well, who does know anyone?'

'Right.'

'I'm baffled by all this. I don't think the truth or anything like it has come out, though what the truth is, I've no idea.'

He found he more or less believed her.

'Mr Harpur, why didn't you ask why he was out of the Volvo? How come something so obvious has to be raised by me?'

26

'Where's your car?' he replied, taking her arm. She did not move. 'I wish you'd tell me how I can help, Celia.'

'That's obvious, isn't it? Just disclose what you know. You seem to be holding back. As you said, why does he bring in that creep lawyer?'

'All sorts distrust the police.'

'I'd heard that.'

'Even when our only aim is to help them.'

She eased herself out of his grip and turned away. 'All right. I'll obviously have to wait until you're ready to speak, if ever.'

'I'll be in touch. Count on me.'

'I'm afraid I don't count on anyone, except my mother.'

'Mine was a right two-timer,' Harpur said.

5

Jamieson's bedside telephone purred and flashed, and he whimpered in disappointment as Street eventually rolled away from him to answer it. 'Yes?'

'Is You-know-who there? This is Simon Wood. The cripple?'

Street sat up.

'This has got to be quick,' Wood said. 'I'm on a hospital pay phone. They're queuing up to tell home about their insides.'

'You sound great, and funny with it.'

'Don't fart about. Who are you? Not Paul Favard.'

'No. Ray Milton,' Street said. 'I work here. I saw what happened. You never had – '

'Just get me You-know-who.'

'I'll try. I think he may be somewhere about the house. Or he might have gone to see his sons. It's his access day, and he never misses, well, you know that.' Street put the phone on 'hold'.

'Wood?' Jamieson asked.

'He sounds shit scared.'

'Blurting from a hospital room, the stupid prat.'

'You want to talk?'

'So he can shout everything on a public line from a hospital ward? What's he trying to do, put me in the *British Medical Journal*? Get rid.'

'He could have information, couldn't he, Cliff – maybe saw them in the Granada.'

'That berk can't tell me nothing. I know who was in the Granada or who sent them and I know who's laughing himself cross-eyed about the forty grand of stuff and I'll have him.'

'All right. But we can confirm, maybe. And he's going to keep on ringing here if we don't do something. He's up to his hair-line in panic.'

Jamieson thought about this. 'Say you'll go and see the bugger, then. Ask his favourite mints.'

Street spoke to Wood again. 'I've been all over the house, Simon, and I can't find him. Like I said – '

'The sod's there with you, isn't he? Where are you, in his pit? Don't I count any longer? Listen, I've been left for dead on his account.'

'I won't say you called. He don't like people coming through on this number except an emergency.'

'It is a fucking emergency.'

'It can get him very ratty, that.'

'And I'm not just people. I want to know am I – '

The pips tore across his words and Street had to wait while he put another coin in.

'Simon, someone will come and visit.'

'Listen, tell him I've got to have protection here. That team know I survived and that I could talk. Anyone could walk in. I'd just have to lie here and watch them.'

'As a matter of fact, You-know-who was talking about protection for you only yesterday.'

'Will he come himself? I mean, this is a bloody big situation.'

'One of our best boys will be there, like me.'

'And pay? I did my side of things. Is it my fault, this cock-up? What chance did I have?'

'Funny you should say. You-know-who was talking about your pay only yesterday.'

'What are you, some sort of bloody answering machine?'

'Seen the Law at all?'

'Yes, he's been. No problems. I gave him a load of ballocks and he swallowed the lot. A heavy called Harpur.'

'Never heard of him, but they're nearly all as thick as shit.' Street put the phone down and lay back in the bed.

'I'd send Favard, but he's got that trouble with his face now,' Jamieson said.

'Extra trouble with his face.'

'I can trust him. Whatever happens I can trust him. That's big, Ray. How many men like that in this game?' He turned towards Street. 'Now, Ray, take it nice and gentle at the hospital. A good look around first. He could have all sorts calling.'

'That's why he's frightened.'

'Fuck him. But you – you go very, very gentle. Make sure you come back – unmarked.' He passed his palm slowly over Street's chest. 'You know, I ought to be in deep agony after what they done to me, but somehow I'm not. You're the somehow, Ray. You give me a lot of joy and calm.'

Street put a hand over Jamieson's.

'So let's make it last, Ray, yes?'

'Yes, oh, yes,' Street replied.

Jamieson gave a sad smile. 'You says that now and you can make it sound good and true, but tomorrow? Them bloody slags you go with, Ray – it hurts. It hurts bad. I never said till now, but it's bad.'

'Well, Christ, you was married. You got kids. How did that happen, then?'

'That's different. That's the past. I made a mistake there, didn't I? You, the way you goes on, it makes it look like you don't give a monkey's for anyone but yourself. That's so selfish, so cruel. This girl, Younger, from the decorator's place. Jesus, Ray, she got to be a slag. All right, she's in a job, but is that going to pay for the sort of habit she got? She tarts. Bound to. All right, she don't make you pay because she likes you, but all the rest do.'

'If I'd known you felt bad about it I wouldn't have got involved,' Street said, climbing out of bed.

'That's what I'm on about, isn't it? If you had some feelings, some feelings for me, I wouldn't need to tell you about it, would I? You'd see it. I mean, look at you now, for Christ's sake. Why the hurry? We ought to talk about things. It's important.'

'Sorry.' Street was dressing quickly. 'I want to see Wood. Where else is he shooting his mouth off? Don't forget I works for you. Someone got to see to these things.'

For a while, Jamieson lay on his back, eyes closed. 'One of them had a Mauser, didn't he, and the others we don't know? You ought to carry something. I mean, all the time now.' He left the bed and opened a combination safe in the corner of the room. He took out a 7.65 FN pistol and checked the ammunition, then returned and sat on the edge of the bed, the gun still in his hand. 'Christ, I hate all this. No, this sort of thing is not for you, Ray. I'll send Favard instead, and never mind his face.'

'They might keep him in. I'll be all right.' He took the pistol. 'Why not try for a kip now? I'll be back in a couple of hours, maybe less. Be in bed still, yes?' He kissed You-know-who on the forehead.

In the bathroom he spent a while rinsing his mouth, trying to be quiet about it.

On his way to the hospital he made his weekly reverse-charge call to his parents and sister, Angela, from a street booth and told them he was on a hopelessly boring administration course at headquarters, never getting out of the office to any action.

His mother said: 'Don't fret, love. At least it's safe.'

'Safe? No. I'm liable to be suffocated by the weight of paper.'

6

At lunch in the senior officers' canteen, Iles was telling Harpur about a number of difficulties in his marriage when a Control Room messenger came to say that there had been a break-in at the flat of Celia Mars, Simon Wood's on-off girl-friend. She wanted to see Harpur urgently, in person.

'Is she all right?' Harpur asked.

'She was out at the time.'

Iles listened but continued discussing his wife when the man had gone. 'We don't talk easily, Sarah and I. Have always humped in silence, as *The Waste Land* puts it. I'd be interested to know whether she chatted much in bed with your colleague, Francis Garland.' Invariably, Iles lunched on a cereal in milk. 'Perhaps he didn't discuss it with you, though. People can be surprisingly delicate when knocking off another man's wife.'

'I'd better go and see this woman, sir.'

'Yes, I don't much like the sound of it. Was she in on things with Wood?'

'That I don't know.'

'Someone could be very scared Wood told her what he saw. He wasn't supposed to live, obviously.'

'I'm not going to hang about, sir.'

'I'll come. You won't mind?'

Jesus.

In the car, Iles said: 'Of course, Sarah and I do *The Times* crossword together. That's our real intimacy, so we certainly do speak quite animatedly. We're not sullen with each other. Nothing like that.'

'Yes, you can get some very flavoursome words that way.'

'I might say, "Try adobe."'

'What does she make of that, sir?'

'She'll reply, "That could give scimitar at 3 Down". There's a kind of contact, you see, an interplay, but it's not really deep. Souls aren't brought together. Yet a man does need that, wouldn't you say? And, Col, she's so thick. On my own I could finish it all in ten minutes flat, but one loiters out of comradeship, like walking home at the same pace with a friend who's pissed.'

'Most women need to be nursed along, sir.'

'But adobe's not what they want to hear when your leg's over. Garland wouldn't have been muttering adobe to her in their sessions at the Exeter. They do like to be told about their beauty and how you love them and will do for ever. I find it a bit tough, all that.'

'Garland's got quite a vocab, sir. Goes far beyond, "Would you kindly blow into this bag?"'

'How could he afford a double room in a place like the Exeter, I'd like to know. Does the manager owe him? What the hell for?'

'Garland never takes freebies.'

'Oh, Mr Bloody Integrity. Well, Sarah must have found some qualities there, I suppose.' For a while, Iles pondered. 'Sometimes, you know, contemplating the sort of life I lead with Sarah, I find myself almost sympathizing with that creature we hunted for knocking off nymphets. There has to be something very attractive about the unformed mind, and the scarcely developed physique – miniature breasts, body hair only just coming through: thank heaven for little curls.'

'I find kids a total turn-off.'

'Bloody liar.'

Celia Mars opened her front door looking very scared. Although she had been clearing up, the flat was still a mess and Iles at once began gathering photographs and pieces of fractured ornaments strewn across the carpet, clucking with distress. 'Dear lady, what a sorrow it is to us, to me, that we fail to protect people from casual vandalism of this kind.' Glaziers were replacing a rear window.

'Mr Harpur, please, what in God's name is going on? What is Simon into? I know I've asked before but, oh, please – '

'You think this is linked with the hit-and-run?'

'I know it.'

'Can you tell whether anything's been taken?'

'Nothing obvious.'

'I'm afraid we see so many lovely homes in this plight, Miss Mars – Celia, may I?' Iles murmured. 'It is no comfort for you to hear that, I know, except that it means you should not feel singled out, not especially menaced. A gang of kids, probably, high on glue and looking for kicks and fivers.'

'Oh, get stuffed,' she replied.

Harpur started to believe that she really did not know anything about Wood's sideline.

'This was a search, wasn't it? Someone turned the place over, looking for something specific.' She pulled open a bureau. 'Look.' Some rings and other small pieces of jewellery had been tipped out of a drawer and left. 'There's a few thousand quids' worth there and he didn't want it.'

Harpur asked: 'So what would he be searching for?'

'They sat among the debris in her living-room. 'You say "he" – one person, a man. Why?' Iles asked.

'Yesterday I was followed home.'

'From where?' Harpur asked.

'The hospital, after visiting Simon. There was another visitor, a young guy, maybe twenty or twenty-two. I wasn't told his name and by that I mean there was a real, special effort not to introduce us. And get this, will you: I had to leave the room while they talked.' She laughed very angrily. 'Simon actually ordered me out. I mean, my God, I'm only there out of softheartedness. He's next to nothing to me now, and I'm told to take a walk.'

'Next to nothing to you now?' Iles said. He seemed very interested to hear this. Celia did look good today, in a mauve, shirt-style dress with a black belt and her dark hair pinned back. Shock and fear made her a little pale, but that suited her lovely, narrow, rather sad face. She might have been an Italian princess mourning over lost terrain. Had Iles suddenly come to see that under-age gaol-fodder might not be the only answer, after all?

'This visitor tailed you?' Harpur asked.

'He waited outside the hospital, and his car was behind all the way here. A Renault. He didn't approach me or anything, and then this. Who the hell is he?'

'Did you ask Simon?' Harpur said.

'He's playing it very tight, I told you. The man's what he calls a "business contact". So, what business? Simon works for an airline, that's what I've always understood. How about you? This business man looks like no business man I've ever seen. They're not going to give him membership at the County Club. He's hard and grubby in a leather jacket, with baby features and cold, two-timing eyes. Did you ever see Richard Attenborough in *Brighton Rock*?'

'A film?' Harpur asked.

'Ah, yes, "Pinky",' Iles said.

Harpur thought he recognized a very fair description of Ray Street. They had given him a hired Renault. 'We can let you see some dossier pictures of villains, if you like.' To Street it would have made obvious sense to look over Celia Mars's place. His job was to get everything that could be got on the trafficking and You-know-who, and if he suspected she had a spot in the firm he would want to take a peep at her secrets. Perhaps he had been half-stoked up again when he created this shambles.

On the way back in the car, Iles said: 'Might this have been our boy, then?'

'Do you mean our undercover man, sir?'

'Age is right. What about the appearance she gave?'

'Nothing like, sir.'

'And one does have to ask whether a trained man could have turned a place into such a tip.'

'Quite, sir.'

'Unless he was juiced up to the eyeballs.'

'His father's a Methodist minister, sir.'

Harpur was driving and Iles sat crumpled against the passenger door. In a while he said: 'I'm thinking of putting a stop to this operation, you know. There's going to be a killing and our lad could finish up with his name and number on the Halo Wall. On top of that, the Chief's picked up an idea that the boy might be getting sodomized as part of his act. You-know-who went queer inside. Not the first.'

'Oh?'

'News to you, naturally.'

'Yes.'

'Well, Lane doesn't like the idea of one of our boys under You-know-who. The burden of poof. I'm not too taken with the notion myself, but you know the pious bloody show the Micks put on about everything except straight-up-the-front hetero, as if monasteries didn't exist. Always ranting about buggers. Think of the Waugh diaries, and he was only a convert. All the same, it's no part of the oath of allegiance to become some powder-pusher's minion. Is he pretty, this boy?'

'Looks like a boot.'

'A young boot. She says baby-faced.'

'Not our lad, sir. We didn't deliberately pick someone repulsive, but he is. Sweats a lot, too.'

'Some like it hot. Look, we could easily finish up with three deads here, couldn't we? Jamieson will be out to get even. And someone might want to complete the job on Wood so he can't talk. Plus Celia Mars, if she's in the picture. I must say it would distress me if any hurt came to her. Who would have thought my shrivelled heart could perk up like this? And all the time our boy could be rumbled and blotted out, especially if he's taking risks like at Celia's flat.'

'His task is to stop killings happening, sir.'

'All right, so tell me this: when can we move, on the basis of what he's discovered? What has he produced that looks like evidence – looks like evidence to us, let alone to a court.'

'I admit it's going to take a while yet, sir.'

'That's what I mean. Too slow. I don't like the softly, softly bit. We've put a lad in a shit pit, Col, and if he gets killed you can bet that some fucking jury will decide You-know-who was only indulging in a nice bit of self-defence, like with Fordham. And police funerals are purgatory. The hymn singing is always so mawkish and rough. Can we reach this kid to get him out?'

'We have a fixed-time meeting, sir.'

'He always turns up?'

Harpur decided on a bit more editing of truth. 'Once he was prevented when driving for Jamieson.'

'Well, next time tell him it's over. Bring him back with you, right? When is it?'

'Four days.'

'Christ, no panic-button drill?'

'From his end, yes. He can reach me if he wants help, but I can't contact him. It would be too dicey.'

'If he's snorting he could give himself away at any time without being aware of it.'

'He's not interested in the stuff.'

'But he might have to get interested if he wants to look real, yes? What do you take me for, Harpur, your bloody aunty or something?'

'No sign he's a user, sir.'

'Never mind. I want him out. Four days from now get him off it and let me know as soon as he's safe so I can officially notify the Mick.'

'The lad is going to be very upset. He's put a hell of a lot of hairy work into this, sir.'

'By which you mean you're going to be very upset. As ever you put your case with great reasonableness and balance, Col, but for once would you just do what you're told when you're told to do it and not stall with endless stupid arguments?'

'It means that You-know-who – '

'Christ, just bring the boy back with you, and not in a body-bag. He's done all he can and shown he's got bottle, if anyone doubted it.'

For a time Iles remained slumped against the door as if asleep now. Then he stirred. 'Could you drive me straight home, Col, not to the nick?'

A sudden surge of lust for a crossword session with Sarah must have hit him, despite the apparent liking for Celia Mars.

7

Over a late breakfast at Nightingale House, Jamieson told Street he was nearly ready to what he called 'break bread with the joker who nudged Wood with a Granada and got stuck to a 40K brief-case'.

'Great.'

'I like to be one hundred per cent sure before I move, and that's the position now.'

'Great.'

'There's a bit of admin first, Ray. You and me can handle that today.'

'So who the hell is it?'

'Don't steam. You'll know soon. You and Paul Favard.'

'Thanks a vatful. Nice to be told my level.'

'You know different.' Jamieson squeezed his arm.

But Street was committed to a bit of sulking and did not respond.

'Ray, I got old habits. Once I opened my mouth too wide and finished up behind a slammer door with a couple of coons for two years.'

'Christ, throwing the bouquets about, aren't you?' Street tantrummed another minute but saw Jamieson would not move. So let it go. A little curiosity was natural, but more might ring bells. 'Isn't it your day for the kids?'

'Drive me. Ray, I want you to meet my children. Now, that's something Favard will never do. You'll like them. And meet Kate, too. You got to think of yourself as family now. We can see to the other things at the same time. I got something I want to leave at her place. Maybe I'll ask you to pick it up in a day or two, so you got to get introduced.' He brought out a thin, flat parcel from his desk. 'These are personal papers, that's all, Ray, but it's wisest if they're not here for a while.'

'Why?'

'Kate'll bitch about the risks but she'll do it for me and give them back, no trouble, as long as she knows you.'

They went up the motorway in the Toyota, Jamieson holding the parcel on his lap. 'See, if things go a bit wrong the law can open a bank box. This is the best way. Look at them fucking fields, Ray. One thing I hate above all it's the country. You ever been on the run in the country? All that sodding mud and they can get dogs behind you like Devil's Island. Give me streets. I never ate a rabbit since then. I know how the poor buggers feel. You still got that FN pistol?'

'Nice weapon.'

'You could need that when we make our visit. Well, what you'd expect. He got some friends close. Friends? No, just hired shit. Nobodies. They got no background. It bother you he got a few bits of rubbish close, supposed to be nannying him?'

'Just I likes knowing what's on my plate.'

'Yea, we'll eat the sods, too right. He got it coming.'

'Where is he?'

'Who, Ray?'

'Oh, Jesus, all right, play games. Am I talking to a kid? Where are we going to make our call?'

'You mean my once-wife's place and the boys? Mill Hill. Big house, there.'

'No, where to when we visits this joker, the one with the happy-time brief-case.'

'Oh, him.'

'Yes?'

'He got a few places he can use, all hovels. He never saw money till now, the ponce. He couldn't afford a place like Nightingale. I'm going to have to find out which one he's at.'

'Yes?'

'Leave that to me, Ray. Don't fret. I'll line it up good.'

'Christ, you mean we don't even know where we're going?'

'We will.'

'How the hell can we plan? We got to know the layout.'

'Ray, just believe in me.'

'Well, I try, Cliff.'

Jamieson turned and smiled at him sadly. 'All I ask, Ray.

Haven't we got to believe in each other? We just got to, you in me, me in you. There isn't nobody else.' He touched Street's hair gently. 'Here's Kate's place.'

It was behind nicely cared for trees and up a wide, curving drive.

'Kate moved to a guy in high tech and legit almost the whole bloody way, would you believe it – as far as I can find out?' Jamieson said. 'That's good. It's good for the kids to be in that sort of house. I would have turned rough if she'd took them to some villain.' He left the car with his parcel and Street stayed at the wheel. 'No, come in. Don't sit there like the chauffeur. You got to meet her, I told you. Didn't I say you was like family now, Ray?'

When it came to the point in court and You-know-who's lawyers were looking for mitigating character points before sentence, Street might agree to go into the box and say he had seen Jamieson being dutiful to his children and former wife. Of course, not long ago he had killed someone else's fourteen-year-old child, among one or two other murders, according to Harpur, so the testimonial to You-know-who's devotion as a family man might fail to wow the judge.

A couple of young boys must have heard the car and came running from the garden to greet Jamieson. Quickly, he handed Street the slim parcel and then picked both children up and held them to him, each sitting on one of his arms. They would be about four and five, yellow haired and blue eyed, like You-know-who, and sturdy and short-legged like him, too. 'Here's the terrible pair I told you about – this is Mike and this horror is Pete. This is Uncle Ray.'

'Where you taking us today, dad?' the younger one asked. 'Is he coming?'

'Of course he is. He's Uncle Ray.'

'What's he got in that parcel?'

'Nothing for you.'

'Why?'

'We'll see about that later, if you behave.'

A cheerful-looking woman of about thirty followed the boys from the garden. She was heavily made, and heavier now, through pregnancy. 'Why, if it isn't the papa figure,' she said. 'I'm the previous.' She grinned at Street. 'Kate.'

'Ray Milton,' he replied. 'Pleased to meet you, Kate.'

'Ray's recently joined the marketing side of our business,' You-know-who said.

She guffawed. 'That what you call it? I heard your business was in for one of the Queen's Awards to Industry for doing Britain so proud.'

Jamieson put the boys down, took the parcel from Street and handed it to Kate. 'Could you hide that in your knickers' drawer for a day or two?'

'Is it your theology degree from Oxford?' She took it almost without protest. 'I don't know what Gerald would say. It could drop us in it, I suppose?'

'Only a couple of days. How is he, anyway?'

The older boy groaned. 'We got to say what's called grace when we're eating. You ever heard of that, dad?'

'Of course I have. That's good. That's civilized.'

'You don't do it.'

'I'm going to learn how. You better teach me.'

'Gerald's fine, I'm fine,' Kate said. 'We get nobody banging on the door at 4 a.m. asking if we'd care to help them with their inquiries.'

'Gives you time for other things,' he said, touching her stomach.

'And you, Cliff, are you fine, too, these days?'

Street thought that for a second the cheeriness went and she sounded sad, as if she missed him. Jesus, but women could be strange. Didn't she know it all about You-know-who?

'Fine,' Jamieson replied.

Street drove him and the boys into Essex, near Chelmsford, where You-know-who had a friend who ran a helicopter-rental business. There was room only for three with the pilot and Street waited for them on the ground.

'You-know-who asked me to have a word with you while the boys weren't around,' Lestoque, the proprietor, said. 'It's about a car. Your department? There's some sort of special outing planned, I hear.'

'Could be.'

'I don't know what and I don't want to, but a bit of a call on someone?'

'Along those lines.'

'Needing a car that's untraceable?'

'Maybe.'

'You-know-who says he'll be sending you over here to Essex for a nice anon vehicle soon.'

'First I heard.'

'You know You-know-who, if you know what I mean. His own little ways of doing things, yes?' They went to a barn where an old blue Ital stood. It looked as if it had been around the world twice carrying the French rugby fifteen.

'Jesus.'

'Only three of you, I heard. Bags of room. There's a decent boot if you got to take anything, well, heavy.'

'Anything heavy would go right through.'

'You-know-who said just something anon, no need for speed or guts. It's only a calling-card job, right? You're not going to be blurting after anybody or making a run, hopefully. So something that can take you there and get you back and won't be noticed or remembered.'

'If it drops its bloody insides on the road it's going to be remembered.'

'I've been all over it and it's beautiful. Am I going to mess You-know-who about? You-know-who I've done work for since – well, since Lady Di was Lady Di. We're like brothers. Some rust, what you'd expect, but nothing terminal.'

'Regy?'

'We're getting plates from a breaker. Another Ital. It's all a nice, tight job, no nasty edges.'

'And when have all you buggers decided I'm going to pick it up?'

'You need to ask You-know-who on that one. Just soon is what I was told and so it's ready when you are. But you know what You-know-who's like about the small print. Well, he's a business man, isn't he?'

'Just tell me if I got this right, will you – I'm going to have to come out to this bloody field in the Toyota, leave it here, take that wreck, go back and pick him up and someone else, make the call, then drive it back and collect the Toyota?'

'Right. You want to chew any one up, you chew up You-know-who, not me. You're a driver? So, drive. We break up the Ital when you return it, that's the picture. Kind of job we're doing all the time. What we call self-sealing.'

'He couldn't tell me all this himself, it's so stupid and long-drawn-out.'

'What I'd do if I was you is leave it all to You-know-who, who does a lot of quiet mulling over matters. You-know-who has seen it all before.'

The helicopter came in. Street's rating with the boys seemed to have improved, somehow. 'Uncle Ray, Uncle Ray, we could see you from up in the air,' Mike called, dashing to him, 'but you were tiny, like a crumb on a cloth.'

'How I feel.'

The other boy galloped towards him, too. They seemed to want Street to pick them up, as Jamieson had, back at the house. You-know-who watched fondly, but Street drew the line at that. Somewhere he had read it was impossible to fool kids. Soft, of course. Kids knew next to nothing and so were easier to fool than anyone. He did not like doing it, that was all.

They drove up to Oxford Street from Essex and You-know-who told Street to lose himself for a couple of hours while he and his sons did a tour of the shops. It was Saturday and from a booth at King's Cross Station he phoned Harpur at home. There was enough new stuff now to justify an emergency call. Not so long ago nobody liked ringing Harpur's house because his marriage seemed right up shit creek and it could be painful if his wife answered. The story was they had sorted something out lately and when Megan Harpur answered now she sounded full of life and even happy. One thing about cop wives, they knew not to ask who was calling.

Street said: 'We're bloody close to moving, sir. A blue Ital, about 1979, resprayed, a very rough job. Plates to come. Two wing mirrors, offside without the glass. Rear-offside aerial. Boot looks as it it has taken a shunt, but OKish now.'

'Who's the target?'

'Haven't got it.'

'Why the hell not? Christ, he doesn't trust you?'

'I think it's all right.'

'What's he playing at? This – '

'I don't believe he smells anything, sir. He says that's how he is. It makes sense.'

'So where's the visit?'

'Don't know that, either. He says he's not sure yet. But no problem. I know exactly where I'm picking up the Ital. You're going to have to watch and follow me. It will be in the next couple of days. There's quite a chance I still won't know where we're going till You-know-who and Favard are with me in the car, like secret sailing orders in the war.'

'Got plenty of coins for the phone, Ray? Do you want to give me the number?'

'It's a credit card.'

'You don't want to give me the number.'

'No need.'

'Did you find anything at Celia Mars's place?'

'Nothing to tie her in. I tried to make it look like kid vandals.'

'You've got a gift for it.'

'Highly beddable lady.'

'Yes?'

'But you missed that, sir? Wood won't be answering her needs for a time.'

'It's not a side of the case I've thought about.'

'Sorry, sir. Your missus in the room?'

'The ACC seemed taken.'

'Really? Does he do it, sir – with respect?'

'He wants to make a come-back.'

'I know all sorts of women who think he's great – a charmer and more.'

'Yes. Listen, Ray, this is not going to charm you: Iles plus Lane say chuck this thing now and return.'

'Well, yes. It's a couple of days, like I said. It will all be tied up then.'

'They mean now, today. The Chief is very concerned about your body.'

'More or less inviolate to date, sir. Didn't I tell you You-know-whose tastes are pretty limited and routine? He doesn't want to go all the way, so far.'

'Iles and Lane still say get out, pronto. And they could be damn right. How come Jamieson plays it so close, telling you nothing when you're supposed to be his pretty boy?'

'No, I haven't had another snort since I saw you. No, I haven't been spilling in my sleep. Listen, Harpur, if he's got any tremors about me it's because someone spotted you at that flat I used, when you broke every damn rule there is. Like you said the other day, you look all cop and nothing but cop. But, not to worry. Let's forget all that, yes? If we do this right we can still have him on toast for attempted murder as well as the trading. He's dumped some incriminating stuff with his ex-wife, by the way, which we could pick up.'

'Attempted? What's that worth, for God's sake? We know he's done three, including a kid. That's what I want him for.'

'But you're never going to get him for them, are you, you dim sod? Where's the evidence coming from? He's got too fly, for you, for Iles, for anyone. We have to grab what we can. With his form, Attempted will be ten. Plus the coke trading. That's another seven or eight. And when we've got him cosy in care we can work on him, can't we – turn him upside down and shake all the juicy bits out? Jesus, Harpur, you mean you couldn't crack him, once we had him in a consulting room? You're getting very modest.'

Street had the one working booth in a group of five and a well-dressed middle-aged couple with very good leather luggage had come from the trains and waited close to the glass for him to finish, now and then doing a bit of peeved pacing.

'So, suppose we could persuade Iles and Lane to keep it alive, tell me step by step how you see it going, Ray. I don't believe you've thought it to the end. All sorts of things could go wrong.'

'Of course it could. Tell me an op where it couldn't. I admit I don't know how it might end. How could I? But I've got to let

You-know-who get as near as I can to killing his target, who-ever he is, and then stop it, or I'm in big law trouble myself, aren't I? You and your team will be waiting close, please, and you come in very quick and very plentiful.'

'What if he's got protection, and of course he's got protection? Are you going to blast that out of the way? Maybe get blasted? This is going to be in a venue you don't even know yet? No recce. Christ, what sort of chance are you going to have? That's if it's on the level. Does it really sound a You-know-who operation, Ray? He's setting you up. I've got to order you to drop it now and get out. Sorry. Where are you?'

'In London, Charing Cross Road.'

'Really. Just get on the tube and disappear. Don't even make contact with You-know-who again. Now, let's be clear: this is an instruction, not a suggestion, and it comes not just from me but from Lane.'

'Fuck Lane, Harpur, I've gone too far with it now. I'm not stopping. I can't. We've got the first likely opening and we back off? Not on. So, listen, this call didn't take place. You never heard from me. I've not been in contact at all. That's the easiest way to solve it, yes? I'm not letting go of him now. OK, so there are things in You-know-who I like –'

'Restrain yourself, sailor.'

'None below the eyebrows. He has an occasional decent thought. But we want him and I'm – What the hell?' The wait-ing woman pulled the door of the booth open.

'Have you taken a lease of this box?' she snarled, in a big, Scots, management-class voice. 'We will not brook it longer, d'you hear?'

Street turned and decided not to hit her with the receiver, but using his free hand struck her a heavy slap across the face, knocking her backwards against her man, and out of the booth. The door swung shut again.

'All right, Harpur? We haven't spoken. If I don't contact you, as far as the ACC knows and Lane you have no way of reaching me for the next four days. So you'll be in the clear with the bosses – your big career, and all that.'

'Ray, you've got to drop it. Don't you understand?'

'No, I bloody don't and I don't want to. I've got a great thing going here. Nobody's ever going to come this close to him again. I'm his sweetheart, can't put a foot wrong. Sometimes I even feel a bastard for what I'm going to do to him.'

'He's conning you, lining you up. Isn't it obvious? They'll probably knock you off at the spot where you pick the car up. Where is it?'

'No, no, I'd sense it if he had smelled anything. What kind of deadhead do you think I am?'

'He's no deadhead, either.'

A small crowd had gathered around the booth. The man was attending to his wife, who had sat down on a case, weeping and trying to put her grey hair straight.

Harpur said: 'How the hell do I pretend I haven't heard from you if we've got to watch your Ital pick-up and tail you? Who told me about it, Ray? You've given up thinking properly. It must be the stuff. Get back here.'

'Well don't bloody watch and follow then. I don't want you or your posse. Leave it to me. I'll get him solo if that's how it's got to be.'

'Ray – '

'Solo. I'm going.'

'Ray, no. For Christ's sake. Where do you pick up the Ital?'

Street put the receiver down and left the booth. 'I'm very sorry,' he told the Scots woman, 'but this was a life-and-death call, you see. My granny is in the hospital and I was arranging to give her one of my kidneys.'

'No damned excuse, no excuse at all,' the man growled. 'I should break you like a stick.'

'May I advise you, laird? Don't try throwing your pathetic bit of Morningside Crescent weight about in London or they'll have your tartan-flecked balls. Now, why don't you get in there to the phone before it's too late and see if your daughter is in from her street beat and can come and fetch you?'

He picked up Jamieson and his sons, each of them carrying a teddy bear wearing red tights and a red cloak. The kids chattered and fooled in the back of the Toyota on the way to Mill Hill, but alongside Street Jamieson was quiet, perhaps depressed that his day with the children was almost finished. Yes, once in a while it did seem rough to Street that he was working for the day when You-know-who would be seeing them a lot less. No, not as often as once in a while.

'Ray, you're not wearing your seat-belt,' You-know-who said.

'That bother you? Such a law-and-order man.'

'Just it's sloppy. Unprofessional. And a bad example to the boys here.'

'So who's a professional?'

'All right, don't get ratty. Not today.'

8

After Street's call, Harpur found himself falling into deep and uncontrollable dread. This operation was jinxed, and any day now it could start going rotten right through. Desmond Iles had been right. He often was. His flair went further than *The Times* crossword.

At night, Harpur went back to the flat in the multi-storey block where he had last seen Street, and found the place cleared. As he prowled the bare rooms with his flashlight masked by a handkerchief, his anxieties swiftly dug themselves in. There was nothing at all left, not even the kind of discarded objects and rubbish that could almost always be found after a removal. These rooms had been very expertly stripped to make sure there were no signs to the previous occupant's identity. The search took him a minute and a half and he did not hang about afterwards. This visit had been a risk, and maybe a mistake, just as Street had said about the one before. Harpur left as unobtrusively as he could, but how unobtrusively was that, for God's sake? The flat had only one door, the front, which opened on to a balcony, like six other front doors. He saw nobody on it, which was not quite the same as being seen by nobody. On the stairs he did not meet anyone, either, not even the venerable, alcoholic tart. People did not wait about these corridors and landings.

In his car he told himself, and half believed it, that to come here and look for Street had been an absolute duty. It was one of the few places where Harpur knew he might be found, and he had to be found quickly. If he was still alive, this lad had big, dark trouble, and did not seem able to realize how big, or did not care, or not enough. He was a kid after glory and if that meant snorting or snuggling up to You-know-who or putting his head in a gin-trap he would do it. Maybe it was because Harpur had recognized these qualities in Street that he had chosen him, and now here was Harpur, out on the road like a clucking, panicky mother in search of a runaway child, and doing bloody badly at it. Oh, where is my wandering boy to-night? Maybe by being seen around Street's place, his ex-place, Harpur was making things worse, but what was he supposed to do, wait in the club until someone reported a corpse?

Jamieson's place, Nightingale House, was a big, turreted Edwardian mansion along the coast, and Harpur drove past it slowly in the hope of seeing Street coming or going and being able to intercept him. Although lights burned all over the house he saw nobody entering or leaving in the few seconds he had to look up the drive as he slowed. There could be no question of loitering conspicuously or calling.

Everything in Street's call stank and everything shouted that You-know-who had him labelled 'cop'. You-know-who had told him no details of their outing because he guessed Ray was feeding his real bosses with all he heard, and guessed right. Who ever heard of a hit-run when the people in it did not know the target, or where the target was, or how they were to get to him? An operation managed like that was almost sure to turn out a bloody mess, and You-know-who had never been in the suicide business. Planning and thoroughness were his obsessions.

It looked plain that Street was being led into position. The supposed outing to deal with this unnamed, unplaced enemy was only supposed, a bit of fiction designed to take Street to some out-of-the-way spot where he could be tidily knocked off. And the more he thought about it the more he grew convinced that it would be at the place where Street had been told to pick up that ageing and battered blue Ital. Christ, how could anyone, even Street blinded by self-confidence, really imagine You-know-who would use a banger? Jamieson would be aware that even the simplest-seeming slay trips could go very badly wrong and that a team might suddenly need some authentic speed and top-class reliability. Harpur would have taken bets that the car was in a remote and fairly distant hiding-place, probably out in the country somewhere around London, but in any case a long way from all spots that might give leads to You-know-who. This kid, Street, alias Milton, was going to saunter out to his execution, thinking himself no-end clever and devious and credible and believing until the end that thanks to his racing brain and rosy lips he had You-know-who beautifully parcelled and ready for the mail.

Harpur knew now that he had handled the phone call from Street like a prize fool. With an ounce more patience and subtlety he could have tickled the location of the Ital out of him. At the start, Street had spoken as if he meant to give it and expected Harpur to be there. Well, of course he had meant to give it, for God's sake. Wasn't that why he had phoned? But then Harpur had jumped in, loud and crude and final, with the stop from Iles, his fucking master's voice. Naturally Street had closed up immediately.

So, if they had not already finished Street, it was on Harpur's plate to find him, very fast. Urgently he tried to list possible routes. Who might know something? There was Wood, there was Celia Mars. Wood might have some notion of You-know-who's thinking, and conceivably the woman did, too. But Wood was in a hospital bed, protected by pity and medics, and it would be tricky getting to lean on him. In any case, Wood had been encouraged to think he was in the clear, just another road statistic, and he must go on believing that: this operation was not a write-off yet, even if saving Street had become the immediate, screaming priority.

Celia Mars? He wouldn't have minded an excuse to visit her

again, although she was a bit lean cuisine. As Street said, she did have something and Harpur was feeling deprived. He and Megan had patched things up at home reasonably well, but only reasonably well.

Elsewhere, Ruth Avery – his sweet, bright, loving Ruth – had decided she should remarry, and since Harpur was not available as a candidate, it must be goodbye to all that. For the past months he had seen little of her, anyway: she put their affair into decline when she met the man now her fiancé, another cop, naturally. Ruth could be very determined and tough. The ceremony was only a couple of days away and, with all the other Force brass, he would have to attend and look pleased. Christ. But Ruth's first husband had been murdered on duty and she had become an inspiring symbol of police resilience. Besides, she had two sons to bring up, and Harpur understood her wanting a father for them, even if he was hurt as a result.

Nor did he blame Celia Mars too much for fancying someone like Wood, a snort courier. He still doubted, though, whether she knew anything about Wood's secondary career, or anything about You-know-who, and he could not risk wasting time with her.

Instead, he thought about another girl, the thin tattooed, druggy, dozing companion of Street, who had been naked and swathed in a table-cloth last time Harpur called at the multi-storey block. In his notebook he found her name, Melanie Jill Younger, and her home and work addresses. It had to be possible that Street was still in touch with her, and she might know his movements for the next couple of days. Street might even be with her, tonight. Didn't the girl keep a picture of him in her wallet? She could be more than just a one-night stand. It must be worth a try.

He drove to her home, a decent-looking flat in a passable neighbourhood. When he rang, a woman's voice answered from a voice box in the porch.

'I wondered if Ray was here,' Harpur said.

'Who is it?' At least it didn't sound as if she was on a dream sortie.

'Business colleague. Rather urgent.'

'He's not here. He never comes here.'

'Oh?'

'Never.'

'I wonder whether I could see you?'

'What for? How the hell did you know to come here?'

'Ray often mentions you, Melanie.'

'You're in the same work?'

'That's it, buying and selling.'

'He in bother?'

'Could be.'

There was a pause and he waited, crouched with his ear at the grille like a history picture of early radio.

'Christ, it's nearly midnight,' she said. 'You should come back another time. I don't like this. We get all sorts around here.'

'It's desperate, love, or I wouldn't have come.'

'I can't help him, can I? I mean, if he's got trouble he's got trouble. How can I help?'

'I think you can. Please. Time's short.'

Again she was silent for a moment. 'It better be quick, and no messing. There's good neighbours here if I scream. We help each other.'

'No messing.' He felt like saying he no longer regarded girls as young as this as within his range. All the same, he remembered with a strong affection her blotto, skinny frame stretched out on the kitchen work-top.

The door opened automatically and he entered a small hall and took the stairs. She was waiting for him on the second-floor landing, wearing jeans, a long navy sweater and no shoes. Arms folded, she gazed down as he climbed the last flight, trying to work out from his appearance whether she would be mad to let him into her place.

'Ray's told me so much about you, Melanie,' he trilled. 'I feel I almost know you. You're a great reader, I hear. *The French Lieutenant's Woman*? Wonderful tale. That by Harold Robbins?'

She led him into her flat, moving athletically on bare feet.

Inside she said, 'Got a name?'

'This is good of you – a bloke just turning up without notice.'

'What's it all re?' She didn't close the door on to the landing. 'I don't want to be late.'

He could see into a small living-room, pricily furnished with modern teak pieces and what looked like a genuine leather suite. There seemed to be some income about. Did mummy and daddy sub her? Did she do a little coke trading herself, with You-know-who as wholesaler? That would knock on the head his original notion that she depended on Street as a supplier. From where he stood in the hall he could see no sign of the habit.

She stood with her back to the wall opposite him, under what might have been an original Victorian water-colour. 'When you say Ray's in bother, what sort?' she asked. 'You mean dangerous?'

'A bit. You know what he's like.' He chuckled.

'Who says so? Who says he's got trouble?'

'If we move fast enough there won't be any. I can promise you that. It's what you want, isn't it, Melanie?'

'So why this trouble? What went wrong?'

'Ray's been a bit stupid, that's all. He upset someone we work with. I'm Ray's friend, so I want to see him right. Obviously, I mean.'

She tensed. 'What do you mean?'

'What, love?'

'His friend. Does that mean – ?'

'No, not like that. We're both girl men. Just his friend.'

'See, there's someone who – '

'Yes, I know.'

'Is he the one giving Ray trouble?'

'Could be.'

'Let's sit down.' She led him into the living-room. There were two doors off it, both shut. She took a chair, sitting on her folded legs. Harpur placed himself opposite.

'Maybe Ray's got trouble because of me.'

'I have to tell you that's possible.'

'This is You-know-who we're talking about?'

'That's right.'

'That shit – he acts like he owns Ray, you know.' She began to shout, and then quietened suddenly, glancing about at the walls as if wondering what the neighbours would make of her outburst. 'You-know-who thinks Ray doesn't need a girl. Ray has to go along with a lot of things with him. You know what I mean?' She was silent and seemed about to cry, her small, pretty face twisted in grief and anger. 'Ray has to do it because of the job with You-know-who. I keep telling him no job is that good. All right, it produces good, this job, but – '

'Can you help me then?'

Her miniature, bony knees were pointed at him. She looked very young, almost fragile, hands clasped together, fingers mashing and kneading. 'What can you do even if you find him? You-know-who's hard, very hard.'

'You leave him to me, and Ray.'

She shook her head and then wiped tears from her face with the back of her hand. 'You can't take him on. Who are you, anyway? I don't know why the hell I'm talking to you, telling you things. You're not in You-know-who's outfit, are you? You don't look to me like someone in the career at all. I tell you what, though – You got a name? You give me your name and the next time I see Ray I'll say you called and you want to help him, and is he interested? If he is, and I don't know whether or not, you can give me somewhere he can make contact, all right? So what's your name? Where can he reach you?'

'Melanie, love, no time for all that.'

'So, have you got a name?'

'When you say next time you see him, when's it going to be? You're sure he's not here tonight, lying low?' Quickly, he stood and stepped to one of the closed doors. Opening it, he found a tiny dining-room and kitchen, empty. He moved to the other door and opened that. There was a bedroom with more teak, everything tidy, and a bathroom and lavatory off. He found nobody here, either.

'You're bloody police, aren't you? I thought you could be as soon as I saw you. Christ, why do I shoot my mouth off?' She hadn't moved. 'I never heard Ray talk about anyone like you, big collar, M & S suit, £1.99 tie. I've seen your kind before, all nice and friendly and full of help to start with, and then the hammer when you don't get what you want.'

'I told you, Melanie, I'm a friend. I'm sorry. I had to have a look.'

'Why's he going to hide if you're such a friend?'

'He's getting so he doesn't trust anyone.'

'Why should he? Where's your handcuffs, copper? What's he supposed to have done? You'll take him in, but I bet your lot won't touch You-know-who, because he's too bloody big and fireproof and hard.'

God, the number of times he had heard that kind of accusation, especially from women. Sometimes he feared there might be truth in it: the bigger they were, the tougher to take them, and it must look to girls like this as if nobody was really trying.

He sat down opposite her again and was saddened for a moment over the way those shiny little knees stuck so tightly together. 'You could be letting Ray drift into bigger trouble, Melanie, much bigger.'

'Can I tell you something, pig? Nobody calls me Melanie. If Ray had really talked to you about me he would have said Jill, not that other fancy name. Jill is what I use. You ever really talked to Ray at all? You got that name from some papers, some pig papers, I don't know what. That was your big mistake from the start. OK, I let you in. Well, I let you in because I needed to know what was going on. Now I know. And you won't be getting one little thing more out of me. I talk too much. So, do you think you could get lost now? Are you in here by trick, without a warrant?'

'You've got this police thing on the brain, love.' He stood up. 'But OK, I've handled this all wrong. You're right there. I made a mistake.'

'Just go, will you. I'm not going to notify the bloody Ombudsman. The quiet life for me.'

'No hard feelings. You've been really decent. I won't forget it.'

She stood, too, now, willing him to go.

Harpur put a friendly hand on her shoulder, preparing to get extremely rough. He wished it was not necessary, but time had begun to sprint and he could no longer mess about. 'Yes, Jill, I can see my mistake here, and I apologize.'

'All right, I – '

'I thought you'd want to help me bring your boy friend back from his deep-throat capers, but why should you care? I'll say this, Jill, it shows a really big spirit to let him take it from his jolly pal one night, and then come back to you the next. Wasn't I dead stupid to think he might be here? He'll be tucked up in Nightingale House with You-know-who, won't he, soixante-neuffing like what's say let's be buddies. They're a true couple, those two, a wholesome credit to queerdom, and you're grand not to resent it.'

Her head dropped. 'Cruel, cruel sod,' she muttered. 'You were setting me up.'

'Tell me: kissing, do you sometimes get the flavour of You-now-who on Ray?'

'Stop it, oh, please, you big pig. I'll yell and call the neighbours.'

'Do they know the nice little arrangement the three of you've worked out? Ray and You-know-who nearly every night in the week but now and then a tiny bit of secret nooky for you, too.'

'It's not like that,' she sobbed. 'No, no, no. Didn't I tell you he got to put up with all that because of the work?'

'Ah, I see. He answered an ad, did he: "Driver wanted. Clean licence essential, also able to cater for special tastes"?'

'He's going to stop. He promised me.'

'Of course he is. And You-know-who's going to let it happen, isn't he, Jill? He's going to say to Ray over the liver and bacon at breakfast, "I hear you've got a charming bit of hetero going and you'd really like to spend all your time there and cut me right out as of now. Well, of course, playmate. Why didn't you ask sooner? Thanks for the memory. Off you go, lad."'

She leaned against the wall, her breathing laboured, no

colour left in her face.

'You OK, Jill?' he asked.

'Look, whatever your name is, and whoever you are, pig or not, I need something. I was trying to crack it, but I've got to have something. I feel bad. I mean, gutted bad.'

'That's all right, love,' he said gently. 'Where do you keep your stuff?'

'So you're drugs squad. Is that what all this is about? I don't give a fuck.'

'If you've got to have it you've got to have it. Was it Euclid or Jimmy Carter who said that?'

She went to the bedroom and he followed. From the wall she took a plain mirror and put it face up on the dressing-table. Then she brought a packet bound with Sellotape from inside a shoe. She put it on the mirror and was about to tip out the powder when Harpur took her wrist hard and stopped her.

'Oh, Jesus,' she whimpered. 'What? I've got to go on now.'

'You can go on in a minute. Tell me where Ray is first. This is his life we're talking about.'

'I'm going to tell you, honestly. His life?'

'I can get between him and You-know-who if you tell me where he is.'

'Is this straight now?'

'Straight.'

'Let me just – '

'Tell me now. Once you've got that in you you won't give a bugger about anything.'

'No, it doesn't hit me like that. Just calm.'

'All the same, tell me now.' He still held her.

She made a weak, hopeless attempt to break his grip. 'You are a cop – and a bastard.'

'Jill, I've got to find him, fast.'

She looked very bad.

'What are his movements, love?'

'He's got to pick up a car.'

'The Ital?'

'You know?'

'There you are. You're not giving all that much away.

Where?'

'It's in Kent.'

'Yes?'

'A little place not far from Tunbridge Wells.'

'Yes?'

'Honestly, I'd remember better if I could get a snort.'

'Remember now, there's a doll.'

'Stapleford?'

'There's a place called Staplehurst.'

'Yes. A farm near there.'

'Has it got a name, as you'd say?'

'Just a farm. That's all I know.'

'Tonight?'

'Early morning.'

'Good.' Harpur picked up the packet of stuff.

'Christ, no, you're not going away with it, are you?'

'What do you take me for, some sort of pig? Is it already cut?' He carefully emptied a nice little dose of coke on the glass and put the packet back in her shoe. As he left she was helping herself from the blade of a nail-file, 'Careful. You've got a lot of money there and you're spilling.'

9

Street felt pretty good. Usually he did feel pretty good. It was a big help. A couple of worries hung about, well, naturally, but nothing that could down him. There had been worries on other jobs as bad as these, and he had come through. He knew how to handle things. They talked about him as a kid, but he wasn't. It made them feel big and capable and compassionate to talk like that, stupid sods. He had told Harpur he would do this job alone, and he could and would, so stuff him. And stuff Iles and stuff the Chief, if he was behind it all, trying to put the stopper in. They were getting old and timid, these big wheels. Even Harpur must be pushing up to near forty. That age, what they thought of not most but always was keeping their nose clean. You could understand. Street didn't want to be too tough on them: they had done it all hard earlier, or they wouldn't be up there with braid. Now they were into rules and straightness. Play safe and God will smile on you with another leg up and a K or two more on your plump pension. Nobody would ever take You-know-who by playing safe because You-know-who knew how to play safe better. He knew how to play dirty while playing safe. The brass wanted him for a fat handful of lumpy villainies, really wanted him, but they did not want him so much that they would take on the risks, even when the risks came nowhere near their own skin. They were leaders who couldn't lead. Yes, age was a savage.

Driving the old Ital alone up from Essex, he would admit it was special, and the testimonials he heard from Lestoque were true, not bullshit. Very kosher magic had been worked on the engine. Of course, you could always bet that if You-know-who had something done it would be done right. Street tried no mad dashing but he could feel the car ready to put on a real spurt whenever he touched the pedal, and he knew the Ital would do it without roaring like Brands Hatch and drawing attention, making folk notice and remember this scrap-yard runner.

Jamieson's efficiency – he couldn't help having a giggle over it. Everything was so great and polished and spot-on, except that the driver was a cop and set to take him in. It would be tough, no question. Jesus, tough, tough. But surprise was worth any number of men and Street felt totally sure he would have complete surprise on this one. If You-know-who had any suspicions or doubts, would he have let him bring the job car alone?

All right, Harpur was panicking and believed the cover might have gone. He probably thought an execution had been arranged around the Ital, among all those blank fields. That would be why he had wanted the location so badly from Jill Younger. Daft bugger. Harpur dreamed all the time of making things one-hundred-per-cent safe and was always on the jibber because he saw disaster about to move in. All the defeats and cock-ups and not-guilty verdicts eventually knocked the guts out of them. On top, Harpur seemed to have something askew in his marriage, so life had filleted him. Street knew he might get like those shagged-out eminences one day himself. So, fight it off and fight them off: keep them from suffocating you with their caution and sadness.

Street had another laugh, this time at the thought of Harpur looking for him and the Ital in Kent. By now he must realize he been fooled. Jill Younger had done bloody well there. He must try to see her soon, not just talk on the telephone. Jill had her weaknesses but he thought a lot of her, and she seemed to think a lot of him, too. It showed a real brain that she could make up all those false directions for Harpur. Women weren't necessarily better than men at lying, but when they were good they were perfect. All the same, it must be another sign of Harpur's decay that he believed her. Why should he expect the truth when he had been so heavy and dirty with her? He meant well, maybe. He'd say that all he wanted was to protect Street, and any method would do. All sorts of oldies meant well and still managed to foul things up good. Meaning well was never going to put You-know-who into Long Lartin.

Harpur and a few good boys could have helped on this coming jaunt, he wouldn't argue. It would have been tough, anyway, and a sight tougher without them. The sad thing was, though, that Harpur and a few good boys were not on offer, because Harpur had orders to close it all down, and Harpur did what he was told, that being what keeping your nose clean was mostly about.

The job could be completed alone, he was sure, though he did not know yet how he would do it. How could he? He still had no details. He had been told it was a calling-card visit and that he would drive. End of information. He could not plan. But what he did know was that he must make his move against You-know-who this time because no other time would be allowed, and when he did make his move he should be ready to deal with Favard simultaneously. He could do it, he could do it. Better with help, sure, but he could still do it. And when it all came out peachy, and You-know-who was deep inside, chrysalized in sentences, they would all be grateful to him for ignoring instructions. Suddenly, then, Harpur and Iles and Lane would go back to rather liking this operation after all, because it would be a winner and over and safe. They loved what was over and safe, and what could be told differently from what it had really been. They felt in control when a case was not awkwardly alive any longer but neatly between the covers of a file, with all the rougher bits left out.

Then, as he drove into the grounds of You-know-who's place, Nightingale House, Street found for a second that he was wishing it all over and safe himself. For half of half a second he experienced a kind of dazing terror. Jesus, he was twenty-two and skipping like an idiot babe into God knew what, on an expedition that looked like suicide even without making his move against Jamieson. If it had frightened Harpur it must be bad. Harpur did not panic. For that half of half a second, Street's foot came off the pedal and he thought about turning around and driving back out and down to Jill Younger's place, or even to headquarters and those high-flying, brass-bound leaders of men. There would be no re-criminations. They would welcome him, and feel comfy again, because he would be back in the nest. They would have escaped the dread that soon they might be organizing a halo parade in his memory.

'Sod that,' he muttered. 'If those three dead-beats like it, it's got to be bad.' He parked and let himself into the house.

Now the car was here and ready, would You-know-who decide he had to give a briefing at last – name, a destination, a hit scheme? And if he did, could Street get a call to Harpur and Iles in time? Did he want to? They would have to respond, but they might do it with deliberate clumsiness, determined to make sure the outing never happened. That was what they wanted, and he would not offer the chance. To think of con-tacting them was mad and weak, part of that crummy dread which had taken hold of him just now, and which he had kicked into the gutter.

Street loved You-know-who's house. He would miss it when the job was over and Jamieson bricked in good somewhere else. He had taste, taste enough to spot the house in the first place, and then not to mess it about. 'Christ, Ray, imagine what some woman would have done to it, even Kate,' You-know-who had said once. Street lived here continuously now, since You-know-who decided the council flat had too many nosey neighbours. Street still couldn't be sure whether the loony visit by Harpur had been spotted. He didn't like thinking about that.

The house had big rooms with boarded floors which Jamieson had sanded himself and kept exposed, except for a scatter of good rugs smuggled in from the Middle East. One of his fiercest criticisms of a house or restaurant was 'all fitted fucking carpets and wall-lights'.

He would usually sit on a straight kitchen chair in a small room at the back of the house where an open fire burned except in high summer, reading the racing pages and books on the Raj, and occasionally staring at the untended garden through french windows. A handsome sundial was almost lost in soaring weeds. You-know-who had mentioned it once, with a trace of shame. 'But I got a Rolex, Ray, and so have you.'

He was not sitting there when Street arrived today. Spread out on the floor was his copy of *Sporting Life*, and an arrow pointing to it had been made on the floor with shoes and slippers. He saw that a message in pencilled capitals was scrawled for him around the margins. You-know-who did not write letters, so there would be no notepaper in the house. 'Paul Favard and I had to go out on the jaunt you may have heard about. We'll be gone two days. I decided I don't want you mixed up in it after all. We took a different anon car but thanks for the Ital. Plenty of meals in freezer. Kisses, Cliff.'

He sat down hard on You-know-who's chair, moving the newspaper around in front of him like a steering-wheel, to read the words again, and almost weeping with anger. The job was stone dead for him, slaughtered by love. In one way Harpur had been clever to see something mad and unlikely in the arrangements for fetching the Ital. They had been a diversion, all right, though not concocted to make a killing ground for the end of Street, but to take him out of the way while Favard and

You-know-who prepared for their card-call visit without him. They must have had parallel plans under way for the real car right from the start. You-know-who was another one who wanted above all to keep Street safe, valued his soul and flesh so highly that he could not let him near the danger. Oh, God why did they all have to protect him?

Street went carefully right through the house, in case the message was some sort of trap and Jamieson still here and waiting to see how he reacted. Perhaps he wanted to know whether Street would get on the blower right away with this new information. The place was empty, though. So, after all, you could believe what you read in the papers, around the edges.

Downstairs again, he did not ring headquarters. Harpur might still be flogging through Kent, looking for him. In any case, what the hell could Street tell them if he did phone? It would sound like farce, the miss of all time, and he would come out of it looking like the fool of all time. That he could not face. His image would be on the line. Until this, he was the brilliant kid who got things right, not some bungling wanker. Best lie low. And something else: Street did not trust You-know-who's telephone. Jamieson was growing fond of gadgets and might have it bugged. Forget Harpur, then. Street might still be able to pull off something when You-know-who and Favard got back. Might. Might? Christ, where had his nerve and push gone? Suddenly, he was beginning to think like Harpur or Iles, like a husk.

If he was going to lie low he wanted someone to lie with and, instead of calling Harpur, he rang Jill Younger. 'How would you like to come over? Stay the night.'

He had not spent any real time with her since Harpur found them both post-coke and thick-nimbussed in the council flat. Now, while You-know-who was away, he would take the chance to prove something to Jill. Didn't she always say Street was scared to be seen with her by Jamieson, and scared above all to invite her to the house?

When Jill answered now she was still at it. 'Stay at You-know-who's place? You've got to be kidding.'

'I'll pick you up.'

'Has he gone on a world cruise or something?'

'Wouldn't matter whether he was here or not.'

'Just happens he's not, though.'

'You make it bloody hard work inviting you, Jill. Look, I'm lonely, that's all.'

Always her accusations pissed him off. All right, they were only to do with a role he had to play, but Street loathed being thought afraid of anything, especially by a girl he was fond of. Jesus, some tangle: on this sort of undercover job he often had trouble keeping clear in his head who he really was. Well, of course. If that didn't happen to you at least once in a while, and if possible more, you'd never be any good. The other life had to take you over. That was one reason he never carried police identification. It would not have pleased Harpur or Iles or the Chief to know that, but Harpur, Iles and the Chief did not have to put their neck on the block.

'Are you calling on his phone?' Jill asked.

'Where else?'

'Couldn't it be – '

'I wouldn't wish to have any secrets from Cliff,' he intoned.

'Well, not too many.'

'Honestly?'

'Honestly.'

'Did you do the job for You-know-who then?'

'Job?'

'Pick up the car.'

'Oh, that. Yes. All neat and tidy. He's pleased.'

'Ray, have you got some stuff there?'

'No chance. Cliff won't have it in the house. Can you bring some?'

'That why you want me there?'

'Jill, I – '

'OK, OK, don't blow your top. But now listen. Are you sure about this – me coming there? Is it safe for Christ's sake?'

'I don't get you. Safe?'

'Safe. If he comes back and I'm in the house. You know what You-know-who is like about women.'

'Stop panicking. I can handle it.'

'I heard.'

'Cliff's away for two days.'

'You could come here. Ray, I do want to see you, love, really want to see you. It's been a long time. But can't you come to my place?'

'No, I've got to stay. There might be messages from Cliff. He'd expect me to deal with them. Anyway, I want to show you the house, don't I? Beautiful. You'll love it.'

'All right. If you say so.'

'And this is the master bedroom its very self,' he simpered, like an estate agent, an hour later.

For a moment she stood hesitating at the door. Downstairs they had both put themselves outside a bold ration of coke and were now close to soaring, but fear could still reach Jill, and for a second she seemed unable to take the extra steps into that special, private, place.

Street himself felt a bit of that fear. God, it was the second time today he had been hit by weakness. To fight back he started pulling his clothes off. 'Come sport with me on and in and around the super king-size.'

She remained in the doorway, though, laughing as he swayed on one leg, getting his trousers off.

'You're piling your clothes up all neat, like a suicide at the sea.'

At once he kicked the heap across the room, so they spread over the boards in a straggle. A shoe which had not moved he picked up and flung into a corner where it crashed against a gilt-framed photograph of some elderly woman, knocking it off a wellington chest and smashing the glass. It could be You-know-who's mother. He had never said who it was and Street had never asked.

'Oh, Christ,' Jill said. She did come right into the room now, wanting to clear up. 'Ray, let's put things as right as we can and then split, yes? He's going to be horribly mad. I wouldn't like to be here.'

But he took her by the hand and tugged her towards the bed. 'Leave the debris, love. We'll patch it up later, much later.' After all the little quaintnesses that had happened to him here, it was suddenly very important to have a woman in this bed, and especially a woman who knew about what went on in it usually. He yanked back the coverlet and turned to her. Gently, he started to take her things off. 'You've no idea what a treat it is to see a pair of tits, Jill.'

'One thing I hate, it's crude talk.'

'Love, it was just my heart singing. I ought to pick my words better. Sorry.'

'Well, all right. As long as you know.'

When Street awoke someone was shaking him hard and before he opened his eyes or cleared his brain properly he thought, Christ, Harpur again.

But it was You-know-who who spoke, and he did not sound too sweet. 'I think you brought a girl in here, Ray, right here, into the bedroom.'

Street heard someone further off working with a dustpan, gathering up glass. He opened an eye and saw it was not Jill but Favard.

'And snorting,' You-know-who said. 'You're still half-stoked. You know I hate that in the house, Ray.'

Street opened his eyes properly. 'How long have I been out? Two days? That can't be.' It mustn't be. Where was the girl?

'No, it was easier than we thought,' You-know-who said. 'That's what comes from decent planning. Dead easy. It was beautiful. We're back early. Tell me now, Ray, you brought some piece of pussy back to my house and into our – into this bed?'

Thank God, she seemed to have gone. Street was in the bed alone. 'Why say that, Cliff?' Jesus, what sort of big-headed lunacy had it been to gabble all that to her on the phone? Had You-know-who been listening to the tape?

'I can smell her, that's all,' You-know-who said sadly.

From the other side of the room, Favard called: 'Looks like they been playing pot shots at your things with shoes. Maybe the screwing got dull.'

'No, an accident,' Street said. He tried to get his head clear, but You-know-who had it right and he was struggling through a coke mist.

'So, what pussy, Ray? Is this some slag from nowhere, the sort I spoke to you about before? Who is she? Where from?'

'You got this wrong, Cliff, I swear.'

'While you're snoring away there, Paul had a view of the sheets. Myself, I couldn't bear to do it, but you think Paul don't know what a bed looks like when a bird been in it with a bloke?' His voice went up to near a scream for a moment. 'This is my bed you been soiling, I suppose you realized that? You wasn't so snorted up you didn't realize that? Or was it an extra kick?' His voice rose.

'OK, I had a snort but no girl, I swear, Cliff. Look, didn't I need a snort? I comes back with the car and finds you've cut me out, left me here. What am I supposed to do?'

'Where did it come from?'

'What?'

'The snort, for Christ's sake.'

'I had some kept back for a bad day. I'm sorry. I know it shouldn't be around the house, but I have to have some handy, just for when I'm down. I was real down. This was a rotten day. I was hellish worried about you, Cliff.'

'Oh, yes, I know you're worried. Yes, it's a bad day. It was a good day, one of the best. We made our visit and left a card, so easy, and then I comes back thinking celebrations and bringing you a good presy.' He pointed to a large wrapped box on one of the rugs. 'And what I finds is this, Ray. You couldn't give a dog's shit what happens to me. So, where's the pussy? She still in the house somewhere sweet dreaming?'

Christ, yes, she might be.

'I'll look,' Favard said.

'There's no girl I tell you,' Street muttered.

'Then come back, Paul. Bring her if you find her. She'll be blotto, but bring her.'

'Right.'

Street raised himself on his arm in the bed. You-know-who was sitting on the edge and gently pushed him back. 'No, Ray, you stay there.'

Street's brain began straightening itself fast now and he itemized possible weapons for defending himself, and defending Jill, if she were still here. You-know-who looked as Street had never seen him before, part rage, part disgust, part disappointment. With these Street could have coped, but there was also a glowing, savage frenzy all over his heavy, fair features. His eyes shone blue and manic. He had killed someone today, it had been a doddle and he had the taste. Favard might be the same or worse, and before he came back Street had to get out of the bed and arm himself. As he was, he wouldn't have a chance.

The training said you could always find something useful and lethal. Not far from the bed hung a wall mirror, which might give him a sword edge if he had time to pull it clear and break it across. Nail-scissors on the dressing-table had hopelessly short blades, and the dressing-table was far off. A straight-backed Victorian chair might do something as a club, but while you were swinging it against one the other would have a lot of time to get you from the back.

'What made you do it, Ray?' You-know-who's voice was down to normal again, sad and flat.

What made him do it? He wanted to show a girl he was not gutless and not a suck, and sod the risks. If those two had stuck to their schedule there would not have been many risks for him, anyway, but he had not allowed for changes. He saw now that maybe there was something kiddish and hasty about him, after all, and it could turn out costly. Just the same, he kept trying to plan methodically how he might protect himself from an attack by the two of them.

'Tell me then, Ray. Do you hate me?' You-know-who asked. 'Did you have to dirty everything, my home, our bed, even a picture of my mother?'

'Cliff, let me get up, will you? I can't think lying here.'

Jamieson shoved him back again. He put his hand inside his jacket, as if to check he had something ready there, maybe a knife, maybe a piece, though he did not produce either. 'Stay there. Think? No need to think. Just say what happened.' He began to get near screaming again. 'So, what the hell hap-

pened, Ray? What you got against me? Didn't I make things
good for you? Christ, I put cottonwool around you and you
reply with this.'

Favard came back. 'Nobody. She've done a bunk, whoever,
she's not so stupid.' He came across to the bed. The wound on
his face was only just starting to heal. 'That's good, keeping
him in the bed. No probs ditching a mattress, but we don't
want no mess on the boards.'

'Now hold on,' You-know-who told him. 'No need for that
sort of talk.'

'I thought you was – '

'Just take it easy, that's all.' You-know-who turned to Street
and shrugged, signalling that only the two of them could really
understand the situation. Favard sat down on the other side of
the bed, very close, almost on Street's legs. All the same, he
reckoned he could still get out to the mirror if he was very fast
and used all his strength. That bloody coke took something out
of you, though, and not just the brain: the muscles.

'Ray, it hasn't got to be like this, has it?' You-know-who
said.

'No, of course not, Cliff.' Despite the terror that held him
hard now, his voice still came out all right.

Jamieson leaned forward. 'Ray, if you can say it again, really
tell me, swear there wasn't no girl here – just if you can say it,
that's all.' His eyes still shone, not with frenzy now but tears.
To go on the slaughter-call he had dressed in one of his finest
navy-blue pin-stripe suits, a dark-blue silk tie and a white silk
shirt, and had come back without a mark on him or his clothes.
He looked like a lawyer. 'What I want is really simple, isn't it?'

'Cliff, I've told you, haven't I? What else have I been trying
to tell you all along?'

'I could believe it, what you said about the picture, that
could be knocked over by accident, if you was snorting. And a
picture: so what? I mean, it's only a bit of glass and cardboard.
Who's going to make a big deal of that, for God's sake? All
right, you been bloody naughty snorting here, you know the
rules, but I can see you could of been having a bad time, being
left behind, I understand that. In a way, that does you credit,

you felt so upset not being near me and able to help on what could of been a tricky one. I appreciate that. So, Ray, if you can look at me now, really look at me, and say no girl, that's all right, we're back like it always was and like I want it. Yes, I know you said no girl from the start, but if you could say it again now, now you been thinking about things, say it like a statement in front of a solicitor, if you knows what I mean, not casual, sort of considered, that would be all right.' He touched Street's shoulder lightly for a moment.

Amazed, Street realized that You-know-who meant it. He still wanted Street so badly that he would believe, or pretend to believe, anything. Perhaps if Street swore there had been no girl, You-know-who could take it as an apology, even as a promise that there would be no more women from now on. He was crawling. Favard looked disgusted, but did not speak. Street gave up the plan to fight his way to safety. An easier solution had been put on offer. He was a brain man, not a heavy, and it would be clever, it would be obvious, to give You-know-who what he longed for, what he was weeping for.

'Cliff, believe me, I would never, ever – '

Now Favard did speak, though. 'I never told you one thing, You-know-who, because I knew it would hurt you bad and there didn't seem no need till now.'

'What the hell you on about?' You-know-who asked.

'He got a girl's lipstick traces on him.'

'Yes?' You-know-who glanced at Street's face and mouth, not seeming troubled, ready to ignore even this plain evidence of lying, as long as they could come back together again.

'I mean down below,' Favard said. 'You know? That's what I meant, it would hurt you, You-know-who. They been oralling. This one don't care anything about anything.'

Jamieson gasped like someone who had been hit hard in the body. Street saw his face change again, now to a mixture of appalling melancholy and feverishness.

Jesus, sweet Jesus, had Street let his chance go, that tiny, fragile chance? Now, now, he had to make his move, and he flung himself forward, throwing the clothes back, and tried to get out on You-know-who's side, reckoning him to be the lighter of the two and the easier to deal with in a hand fight. And it worked. Christ, it worked. If you had a go, didn't cave in, it would always work. That was his gospel, the gospel of the still-young. Street hit You-know-who with a heavy right in the face as he forced himself past and got his feet on the floor, then ran naked for the mirror.

'See? Lipstick,' Favard shouted.

'Can't you shut up, you bastard,' You-know-who yelled at him.

Street had his hands on the frame of the mirror and was tugging it from the hook when he saw in the glass You-know-who standing behind him, still near the bed, a big, red patch on one cheek from the blow. He was holding a silenced revolver two-handed and aimed at the back of Street's head. In the Ital, Street still had the pistol You-know-who had given him, another crazy error.

He howled. 'No, Cliff. She meant nothing, nothing. Only you, I swear.' Street heard him sob in a kind of reply, but then came the mild crack of the gun and before Street fell dying he saw his blood and bone on the mirror glass as it shattered and went down with him.

10

There was a big and joyous turn-out for Ruth Avery's wedding, and the Chief found a way of meeting a big slice of the reception costs at the Martyr. Lane, like Barton before him, was hot stuff on welfare and had a way with public relations, too. Local television came, and the Press. This rated as a very positive story for the police: a widow whose officer-husband had been murdered was marrying another officer.

It all gave Harpur heavy grief, but he had to go, had to behave decently, had to make himself look a cheerful part of a fine, triumphant occasion and wish her and him well. Luckily, Ruth and Harpur had always used down-market hotels, nothing in the Martyr class. He didn't want some receptionist recognizing him and assuming he was the groom.

She had bravely rebuilt her life after tragedy, the minister said, and deserved all the happiness and security that this marriage to Robert would surely bring. Who could argue, and Harpur smiled and nodded, exactly like every other guest in the chapel. In fact, he was exactly like every other guest in the chapel now, a spectator, with no special route to Ruth. Harpur's wife turned and whispered to him that Ruth looked radiant and seemed to mean it, though she might just have intended to do him injury. Harpur had never worked out how much Megan knew, how much of the job gossip had reached her. Anyway, it was true that Ruth looked radiant, and it did hurt.

He felt almost pleased that he would not be able to stay long at the reception. The four-day routine meeting with Street was due at 5 p.m. and there could be no question of missing that. Without fail he must bring him back today. Iles and Lane had grown more and more edgy.

Of course, this supposed Street turned up. If he was still playing obstructive and still chasing glory he might not. What could Harpur do then? It would be impossible to conceal any longer Street's rejection of orders and the shit would start to fly. Most of it would home on Harpur for creating this situation in the first place. Maybe the arguments against using kids were better than he had ever admitted. Yet who but a talented kid could have got on living-in lad terms with You-know-who? It was important to look for a target's weaknesses, and to exploit You-know-who's a pretty boy was needed, not some gnarled thug with service back to Peel.

Ruth and her new husband came down the aisle arm in arm and beaming, her sons and his daughter behind, grinning, too. It had to be a good thing, surely, something really open and wholesome. Ruth saw him, met his eyes and kept the same general, all-purpose smile, the same all-round look of happy sweetness and contentment. Then she turned her head away. Maybe a minute too late he summoned up his good loser's face.

At the Martyr bar before the meal and speeches, Iles put his wife, Sarah, and Megan to talk, and then said to Harpur: 'Haunches, an inner warmth, noble skin, Mensa-plus mind I hear, but supremely the haunches – of course you're stricken at the loss, Col, and you look it. Try and brighten up, do. It's a wedding, you know, not a cremation. Strive to see your part as a task fulfilled. You held Ruth together in difficult times.'

He wanted to escape this. 'Are you getting anywhere with Celia Mars, sir?'

'Celia? A delight, Col. We supply a need in each other.'

'I'm glad.'

'You understand these things, Col.' He would not be diverted. 'I want you to know it was selfless of you taking therapy to Ruth night after night, in the way you did. And I've never heard it proved that your obsessive playing around there compromised your police work, certainly not fully proved. You did damn well, and don't think it's unrecognized. Now, thanks to your warmth and consideration, here she is, reconstituted and hearty, able to go her own way again. It's a personal triumph for you – not a Queen's Police Medal matter, but distinguished just the same. What's that sod doing here, gatecrashing? I particularly checked he was not a guest before bringing Sarah.'

Francis Garland, wearing his usual green-tartan duffle jacket and no tie, had appeared and stood near the door, scanning the crowd.

'Weddings,' Iles snarled. 'People at their worst. Sex festooned in rigmarole. Manias are stoked. Look at the bloody viciousness in that face.'

Harpur crossed the room to Garland. 'Are you here to strip and ravage Sarah Iles? Again?'

'Can you come outside a minute, sir?'

This was the best chance of escape yet and he gladly left the atmosphere of gaiety and congratulation.

In the foyer Melanie Jill Younger was waiting, seeming very distraught. She wore an old raincoat over jeans and a sweater and had looked much better in a table cloth. Guests still arriving from the chapel pushed past, noisy and high-spirited.

Garland said quietly to Harpur: 'It's about Ray Street, or

Ray Milton, as she knows him, so I thought you'd better hear soonest. I've told her your name.'

'Mr Harpur, I'm sorry about sending you to Kent, honest I am. You'll never know how much. I hope you didn't waste too much time?'

'Some. A lot. It was the wrong place?'

'Look, it's just a habit with me not to help police, you know. Yes, I got too many habits.' She was shaking but said: 'Don't take any notice. I'm thinking straight, regardless. Something has maybe gone real bad because of sending you the wrong way.'

They found an empty conference room and sat down around a big, polished table. 'What's bad?' Harpur asked.

'The thing is, I've been trying to contact Ray and I can't find him. Look, Mr Harpur, I don't care now if you do get him for whatever it is. Lock him up if you want to. But it got to be quick, which is why I went to the nick. I don't know what trouble you were talking about when you came to my place, but now he's got real, real trouble.'

'Oh, don't panic, Jill,' he said. 'We'd heard he was going away. That's what the car's for. Of course you can't reach him. He's not around for the moment.'

Garland said: 'There's more.'

'He didn't go. He was left behind, and the car. I've been there with him while You-know-who was away, and I took the phone number when I arrived, another habit. I was so scared about him that I rang up today because I hadn't heard anything from Ray, and they said he wasn't there, not just like he wasn't there, but like trying to talk as if they'd never heard of him, and they're trying to find out who I am and how they can find me, you know? Maybe I shouldn't have rung, but I couldn't forget him just lying there snoring, could I? They seemed to know I'd been there, though I swear they never saw me.'

Harpur grew alert. 'They didn't see you, but you mean you saw them?'

'They woke me up, coming back.'

'Who?'

'You-know-who and that other one, his sidekick. They're

laughing and joking and shouting so much it reaches me, even in a coke doze. I woke up sleeping on the stairs in Nightingale. If they'd come up they would have fallen over me, simple as that, not a stitch on, and I don't think I'd be talking to you now. But it's lucky, they're yelling and giggling downstairs in the big hall, sitting on a bench there for a bit, laughing together, it's a huge, ugly place. Ray likes the house, but you can stuff it, brown paint everywhere, brown benches like in a church in the hall. And all that bloody coloured glass in the windows and the door, like a church, too. The stairs are like in a palace, with a turn in them, or they could have seen me from the hall. Thank God I had my clothes near and so I'm dressing fast, dressing lying down on the stair carpet, afraid to stand up, and they're still carrying on downstairs, the front door open, and in and out of their car bringing a couple of cases and a parcel or two and saying they've got to tell Ray how easy the visit was and how he'll be so upset he wasn't there, but they got a present for him, a great present You-know-who says, that's what's in one of the parcels, and it's going to be such a great surprise for Ray, he'll love it.

'And they're calling him and wondering where he is, why isn't he there to meet them and all that, and saying he could be out, but I know where he is, he's in the bed and far, far away, he took more than me. He was really down and needed something, he was bad because they'd gone and left him behind. I thought he was lucky because from what I could make out it might be a bit dicey, but he really wanted to go. So he was snorting to forget the disappointment.

'Me, somehow I knew not to snort too much that day, I didn't like being in the house. So I came to in time, thank God. And You-know-who is downstairs and sometimes not laughing but sounding worried, saying he thought maybe Ray had gone oïf real angry because of not being taken on the trip with them. So, they go into some room at the back, still calling him, and the front door's open, there must have been some more cases to come in. So, I've got to decide smartish, stay or get out. What good if I stayed? It wouldn't do Ray no good even if I could wake him up on the quiet and warn him. You-know-who's not going to be a bit pleased to see a girl in the house with Ray. So when they're still in this back room and I think making tea, I heard a kettle, the kitchen could be that way, too, I start to get down the stairs, I thought it best to get out while I could. I decided it's best for everyone, especially Ray, which is the important thing. They might never know he'd had a girl there, that was the best. I still think that was best.' Her voice rose as the doubts and agonies welled.

'I'm sure it was, love,' Harpur said.

'Bloody good thinking,' Garland added. 'When was all this?'

'Day before yesterday. Maybe I should have come to you sooner.'

'It's OK,' Harpur said.

'Well, I'm down the stairs and out, holding my shoes in my hand until I'm right down the big drive. And I really made sure there's nothing left where I'd been sleeping on the stairs, no bits from my handbag or anything, and I got all my underwear on, I really checked that when I got home. So, maybe they wouldn't be able to tell he'd had a girl there. But you can see why I'm real scared, Mr Harpur.'

'It could all be OK,' he replied, his mind clothed in black.

Garland's mind kept operating well, though. It usually did, thank God. 'When these two were talking and laughing, Jill, did they ever say where they'd been – name a place?'

'Why?'

'It could help us.'

'But is it going to help Ray?'

'Just try and think, there's a good girl,' Harpur said. 'We'll get moving on Ray, don't worry.' And by Christ they would.

Garland went on, 'Like, when they said it was a pity Ray hadn't been with them on the trip, did they just say the trip or was there a word in front, or after – say, "the London trip" or "the trip to somewhere or other"? See what I mean? Can you think back? The word might be in your head somewhere, love. See if you can get it out for us.'

'No, no place. I didn't hear of no place.'

'Or any other name,' Harpur added. 'The visit: did they say who to? Or when they were going on about how easy it had been did they say what had been easy? We've got to know where they'd been. It would help us all, Ray included.'

'How do you mean?'

'You know, people say something was easy and then sometimes they pretend to do it all again, acting and fooling,' Harpur replied. 'Anything like that?'

'Say shooting someone,' Garland suggested, and held his hand in the shape of a pistol. 'Like an execution.'

'Shooting someone?'

'Whatever it might have been,' Harpur said.

'Or knifing.' Garland stabbed the air.

'Jesus, is that where they've been?' she asked. 'I guessed it was rough, but killing?'

'We don't know,' Harpur replied.

'But what about Ray?' she said.

'You're really stuck on him, aren't you, Jill?' Garland asked.

'Maybe I am. I don't meet many blokes like that, and I want him back. Please, I do want him back. He was helpless in the bed, really closed right down. I don't wear scent or anything like that but these gays got noses and hate-buds that can pick up the trace of a woman like a dog with a rabbit. And he knows about women, he wasn't always queer.'

Harpur said: 'I gather You-know-who's very fond of Ray. He's not likely to hurt him.'

'Well, he's very fond of him as long as Ray is there waiting for him, all nice and faithful and loving, not girling while the master's away. You heard of jealousy at all? Well, You-know-who's into jealousy in a big way.'

Suddenly, Garland leaned across the table and took her wrists in a hard grip, pulling her arms straight and making Jill face him squarely. 'Try and remember if there was any name, any name at all, will you, you chattering little cow? What trip? See if you can hear it again. Maybe they said, "What a pity it was Ray couldn't come on the" – on the what trip, Jill? They're shooting their mouths off, full of themselves. Are you sure they didn't let a name slip while they were patting each other on the back?'

She was silent, looked once at Harpur for help against Garland, and then back to Garland when Harpur did nothing. They watched her think. Then she said: 'Gandhi?'

'The Gandhi trip?' Garland asked angrily. 'Gandhi, for Christ's sake? Do you think they'd been out at the fucking pictures?'

'There was a name like that. Is this stupid? Yes, Gandhi – yes, like you said, that's the funny bloke in the film, isn't it? Or maybe Sandy? That's a name, a pet name, yes? A couple of times I heard something like that in all the laughing. They were shouting something like that to each other, I remember now.'

'Could it be Dandy?' Harpur asked.

'Dandy? Could be that, I suppose. What's Dandy then? That's someone who shows off with clothes? You know someone called that?'

'And they're laughing because they say it was easy with Dandy?' Garland asked. 'That right?'

'Well, it could be. So is this Dandy dead or something? Is this going to help Ray? That's all I want. These bastards will take him away from me if they can. Don't let them. Look, Mr Harpur, talking of Dandy, what the hell you sitting here for in a penguin suit when Ray could be – Well, you don't give a sod, really, do you, because he's a villain, some sort of villain, I don't know, so his life doesn't count, I suppose? Look, just for me, can't you find him and look after him? I'll make sure he behaves right from now on, no villainy. I'll do it, honestly.'

'I'm hoping to see Ray in a couple of hours,' Harpur said.

Garland released her. 'You've done really well, Jill.'

'See him? Yes? Can I come? Who says he's going to be there?'

'It's possible,' Harpur replied.

'How can – '

The door of the conference room was shoved violently open and Ruth, in her plum-coloured silk wedding suit and plum-coloured wide hat, came in at a rush. 'Oh, Colin, I was afraid you'd left. We're just going into the meal. I don't want to be alone in there.' She looked about, confused to see Jill Younger and Garland. 'I'm sorry to interrupt, but I was really scared

77

you'd gone. Please do come in. Don't leave me by myself with them.'

Even Garland took a second to recover. Then he said to Jill: 'Well, we don't need to hang about now, do we? Mr Harpur's got the message, and so have I. We'll work on what they say, Jill.' He stood, took the girl by the arm, drawing her up from the chair, too. They prepared to leave.

'Have a discreet look at Arnold Lorraine's place, Francis, will you?' Harpur said.

'Is that Dandy?' Jill asked.

'That's Dandy,' Garland replied.

Harpur said: 'I don't want you to go in. Nothing sledge-hammer or through the sewers at this stage. Just observe.'

'You the bride, by any chance?' Jill asked.

'Well, yes.'

'What did you mean then, you don't want to be alone in there? Alone? Isn't your husband there?' Jill shrugged. 'One thing I hate it's weddings. Always the wrong people getting together. How does that happen all the time?'

Garland took her out.

'I've got to leave soon,' Harpur told Ruth.

'All right, but just be there at the start, will you, Col? I need to be able to see you.'

'Ruth, you should be – '

'You understand why I'm doing this, don't you?'

'You're going to be very happy, and the boys.'

She gave that big public smile again and held it. 'Robert's a great bloke. Well, you know him. You know he is.'

'Of course.' They stood staring at each other, the table between them.

Iles put his head very apologetically around the door. 'Cries of "Where's the bride?",' he said gently. 'The Chief's banging his knife and fork the way Micks always do when someone mentions free nosh. Let me escort you, Mrs Cotton, would you? Perhaps Colin should wait a few minutes after we've gone. My mother always said tact costs nothing. You'd both have quite liked her.'

Sitting with Megan at the meal, Iles and Sarah opposite,

Harpur felt he was idling. Jill Younger's plea for fast action
gnawed, while he tried to get down *coq au vin* with a white wine
Iles said had to be Asda, it was so fine. Harpur drank very
little. Pretty soon he might need his brain in the sharpest state
he could manage. God, let Street turn up for the rendezvous,
so that a little could be salvaged even from a day when Ruth
married someone else. His fears were at full gallop, he recognized that. The lust to bring in Jamieson at last and do him for
something, anything, to settle for the kid killing and the rest
had shrunk and withered. Nothing counted but to recover
Street.

Sarah Iles said: 'Such a tragedy, don't you think, that the old
Chief didn't live to see this marvellous day? Barton was a fart in
the bath, of course, but he really could be caring.'

Iles groaned. 'Caring? Isn't that a bloody Gerald Kaufman
word?'

'You do hate to hear police accused of decent feelings, don't
you, Des?' Sarah replied. She was in a very winning powder-
blue trouser-suit and Harpur could see why muttering adobe
to her might not always fit the bill. 'You know very well you
worry yourself ragged thinking about the troops and their fam-
ilies. It's very sweet, the most sexy thing about you, after your
recitation from "In Memoriam".'

'Our troops know how to look after themselves,' Iles said.
'They don't need a Mother Teresa.'

Harpur desperately wished that was true. In his speech, the
bridegroom, Sergeant Robert Cotton, was talking about his
new family, which would exist within that larger, warm police
family. The Chief, sitting near him, beamed and nodded like
grandad. Lane had done well to integrate himself so well so fast
within the Force. Cotton spoke admirably, just enough piety, a
nice ration of jokes, and all Harpur could think of as he half-
listened to him and watched her was the two of them chasing
each other around Ruth's big bed in Canberra Avenue tonight,
last night, the night before, tomorrow night and into at least
next month. After that there might be a chance with her again
if what had just happened in the other room meant anything,
and of course it meant something. What Harpur and Ruth had

didn't just die because of a think-of-the-kids marriage.

Ruth avoided looking at Harpur now but gazed approvingly up at Cotton as he said his piece from notes, a decent enough, cheerful low-flyer, one of Nature's sergeants. Harpur stood.

Leaning across the table, Iles asked quietly: 'Crisis? Garland brought an emergency?'

'Nothing much at all.'

'Is it – is this some bother with our lad?'

'Which lad is that, sir?'

At the rendezvous point with Street he waited only half an hour, a coat over his wedding finery, and when he did not show drove home to change, then went straight to You-know-who's place. This time he turned into the drive and stopped outside the main door. A couple of cars were parked there, but no Ital. What was the other vehicle mentioned in Street's notes – a Toyota? No sign of that, either. It was going to be sticky here. How much of what Jill Younger said could be believed? She admitted she made a thing of lying to the police. He still could not be sure how much You-know-who knew about Street, and Harpur must do nothing to suggest this was a panic trawl for a missing cop. He rang the bell and You-know-who himself came to the door in a navy yachting jersey and ball-bulge jeans.

'Routine inquiry, Cliff. You're looking damn well. All aboard for a trip around the bay. And they say cell shadow never leaves the skin. Rot.'

'Mr Harpur! This is grand! And how's your lady wife? And so on? Won't you come in? Paul,' he shouted, 'be useful and bring some drinks into the den. A famous guest.'

They went to a rear room overlooking a wilderness and You-know-who indicated an easy chair for Harpur and took an upright one himself. In a moment the drinks arrived. 'You know Paul Favard?' Jamieson asked.

'What happened to his face?'

'Ask him. He talks.'

'What happend to your face? You're not married, are you?'

'Accident with a lawn-mower,' Favard replied.

'The thing is, Mr Harpur, Paul thought he heard the grass cry out as he cut it and he bent down to listen and speak words of comfort because he got a real streak of tenderness, our Paul, and sees feelings in all life, it's a nice thing about him. But he didn't switch off first. This was at his aunty's place. He spends a devil of a lot of time taking care of his aunty. I won't allow grass-cutting here myself, as you can see. It's my way of backing Greenpeace. What routine inquiries, then? Whisky and water? Say when.'

'More. I'm fond of this place. It's a credit to you.'

'I like to preserve, and in my small way take a share of, the fine things of the past.'

'We've got a nobody called Simon Wood in intensive care after a road accident, multiple breakages, touch-and-go for a couple of days, the usual tale. His girl-friend wants action. Barrack-room lawyer type? So, we've got to move a bit. Well, we had a report of a car with someone in the passenger seat looking possibly like Paul near the scene, but before the carving, I think. This would be a Toyota.'

'Oh, this sounds damn unpleasant. We'd be very glad to help you in that kind of case. Paul, have you been out with friends, banging into folk with a Jap job and not mentioning it?'

'Toyota?'

'That's a new one on us, Mr Harpur. It does look like mistaken identity. I've had the same thing happen to me before. When was this, then?'

'I've got the date but I'm afraid it's going to turn out to be a day Paul was at his aunty's listening to the whispering grass.'

'This is a hit-and-run?' You-know-who asked.

'Something like that.'

'Do you usually handle that calibre of inquiry, Mr Harpur. A bit humdrum for you?'

'We're very interested in finding the driver.'

'The driver? Well, of course. Did your report say what he looked like? If it's a he.'

'We've no details at all. Who else works for you these days, Cliff?'

'Mr Harpur, haven't I told you, there's no Toyota here?'

Jamieson remained composed, sipping sweetly. But then, he

had handled a lot of very tough police questioning in his time, without the aid of Scotch.

'I'm afraid we've been slack and our calf-bound biog of you is rather out of date, Cliff. We've got Paul as a long-time associate, naturally, but nobody later.'

'No, it's not out of date. There's only Paul. Do I need a staff? I'm not GEC. It's only a little property business.'

'Yes, but leaving staff aside, who's reaching your soul these days, Cliff? Who's pouting for you?'

You-know-who got up. 'Well, I'd say I've answered everything pretty good, wouldn't you, Mr Harpur? I've been decent and conversational, offering malt. But you've hardly touched it. Sick? Guts sour? Self-accusation? As I see it, you can't rest, can you, because you never tied me to that kid killing, God knows how long ago?'

'And a few others.'

'Bloody dirty lies, the whole lot, Well, I've got used to this sort of harassment as part of life. Someone pisses through the lord lieutenant's letterbox, so you send the SPG round to find what I was doing at the time. I suppose I ought to hit back once in a while, like the spooks. They give your lot a nice touch of heat up Tottenham et cetera, yes? The Met won't be throwing their weight about in that manor from now on, will they?' He drank contemplatively. 'But, look, I like the quiet life and you got your job to do. I'm on the bloody records for ever, and who can argue with technology? Ask the computer who you ought to question and out pops my name nearly every time. So, here I am, all cooperation and give and take.'

'I'd like to look around the place.'

'Warrant?'

'No warrant, Cliff.'

He laughed aloud. 'So, what the hell? Who cares about bits of paper? Go wherever you like.' He began tending the fire, as if wholly unconcerned about Harpur's search. 'You won't want us peeping over your shoulder. We'll wait here. Don't lift any gold bracelets: I contribute separately to the police Widows' and Orphans' Fund. Going to be looking for a Toyota in the guest bedroom?'

Yes, what would he be looking for? Just any sign that Street might have lived here, and might have died here.

The stairs were as Jill Younger had said, with a turn in them that could have concealed her from the hall, so there must be a chance that the rest of what she said was true.

He prowled the bedrooms, taking his time in the largest. For a couple of minutes he sat on the bed and gazed around. Several thousand pounds worth of what looked like a new, hand-washed Chinese carpet in blue, gold and cream covered almost the whole floor. It struck him as out of key with the rest of the house, which was all sanded boards and rugs: what Alexei Sayle would call "fucking Norway". Harpur walked to the edge of the carpet and turned it back as far as he could without lifting furniture. The sanding was not just a border job but continued for as far as he could see. So, why the cover-up? To lift the carpet properly would have meant moving out the bed and two huge early Victorian presses, plus a handsome wellington chest, and that was not on today. If things continued bad in the search for Street, though, he would come back with a warrant and some removal lads.

Opening the presses, he found only gear that obviously belonged to You-know-who, smart, very expensive, very colourful. In a drawer of the wellington, among ornate cuff links and belts, lay a metal-framed picture of a chintzy-looking old lady. The frame lacked glass.

He wandered through the other bedrooms, opening drawers and cupboards, but finding nothing he could associate with Street. In a small front bedroom papered in subdued red flock, he spent a while admiring a magnificent brass antique inkstand, which had been lovingly looked after and cleaned. A very slim, tasselled silver pencil was lying on it. Harpur picked this up. What he took to be You-know-who's initials, CCJ, had been inscribed on one side. Perhaps it was a present from the old lady in the photograph. Wherever the pencil came from, there could be no doubt that Jamieson liked surrounding himself with beautiful objects and would need a steady, fat income. Harpur replaced the pencil on the inkstand.

He returned to the main bedroom and toured it, this time

carefully examining the walls, but discovered no marks and no evidence of recent cleaning. As he rose from one of these inspections he found himself looking into a nice piece of antique mirror and saw that behind him You-know-who was standing in the doorway watching. He still seemed totally at ease. Harpur turned. 'A ducky room, Cliff.'

'They knew about proportions in them days, didn't they, Mr Harpur? When they built a house they built something to bring you a touch of grace and dignity. This kind of room, every time you enter, you feel you just got to live up to it, act with style.'

'You know, Cliff, I don't think I ever heard lads-together frolics described like that before. It's an eye-opener.'

'Ah, still the same old prejudice and viciousness. Love's not just about having a widow on the side, you know. Will you be able to go on hanging your hat there now she's re-married? But Cotton's only lowly, I hear. Pull rank?'

Harpur nodded towards the carpet. 'The new boy a Chink? Was the special carpet bought in his honour?'

'Oh, that? Picked it up for a song at auction. I thought I might as well get some use.'

'Which auction would that be, Cliff?'

'Are you looking for bargains yourself, then? When I say a song, I mean cheap for what it is. It was still pretty dear, I'm afraid.'

'Beyond me? Sad, that.'

'Don't kid me. You love living down-market: daughters at a bloody comp, and staying on in that dead-beat street. So, that's the image you want.'

'It's my wife. She's very slummy, and she's turned the kids that way.'

That night they found Street. Harpur tried to reach Desmond Iles by telephone with the news at 3 a.m. but thank God he was not at home nor in headquarters and, with any luck, someone else would have to break it to him.

Harpur must have sounded surprised when Sarah Iles said

her husband was not in. 'He's allowed out by himself in the dark, you know,' she told him sleepily. 'Any message?'

'Thanks, no.'

'Big secrets, I suppose.'

Harpur had to call Lane, instead. 'He's at Dandy Lorraine's place, sir. In an outhouse. Lorraine too. They're both dead. Shot in the head. Pistol wounds.'

'Lorraine?'

'He's a trafficker – in a bit smaller way than You-know-who, but tidy enough.'

'Are you saying they shot each other?'

'I'm saying they're both shot, sir.'

'Any weapons?'

'Oh, yes. In their hands.'

'I'll come now.' The duties of a paterfamilias did not shut down at 5 p.m. 'Who found them?'

'Francis Garland and myself.'

'Why were you at Lorraine's place in the middle of the night?'

'We were given a bit of a lead, sir. Perhaps I could tell you about it later?' Yes, perhaps.

They liked a touch of style, these drug-runners. Harpur was learning something about the species. There was You-know-who in his suburban Edwardian mansion, full of pretty furniture, and now Lorraine, dead with Street in a crumbling, windowless lean-to at his country spread, with views from the house over cattle pasture and a small lake towards the sea. Garland at once declared the house Georgian. It was not very big or very handsome or very well cared for, but pretty good for a bit of recidivist rough like Dandy, who went through long, barren times behind the wall. Called Brookside, it stood at the end of a half-mile, pot-holed dirt-track off a minor road, a nice place for the quiet life, and not bad for a noisy death, because nobody would be near enough to hear.

After his calls to the Control Room and Lane, Harpur sat for a moment in what Dandy would probably call the drawing-room. Garland was still with the bodies, trying to sort out what happened, using only a couple of flashlights. Harpur decided to wait until the full murder crew and their equipment arrived with the Chief. He was keen to find reasons for spending as little time as possible with Street's body in that filthy, mud-floored shed, reeking of some chemical stored in sacks. The Chief and Iles would take their share of the blame for the boy's death, but they did not know him – did not even know his name.

It had been an impulse to come out to Brookside tonight. Earlier in the evening, Garland had looked into Harpur's office to report very little joy with his inquiries on Lorraine, following Jill Younger's tip. 'As far as I can make out, he hasn't been seen around for a couple of days. A nark I use up that way thinks there's been some trouble between Dandy and his little crew – the couple of villains who run with him and do the heavy stuff. Could be a row over a share-out. Dandy seemed loaded last time seen.'

'Proceeds of the hijacked Wood delivery?'

'Well, my nark says Dandy did do some sort of job not long ago and he doesn't know what. The blinds are all down around his property and he doesn't answer the door or phone calls. But his motor's in one of the barns.'

'We ought to go and take a look.'

'I think so, sir.'

'Did the nark know exactly when Lorraine was last seen?'

'Two or three days ago. That was the nearest he got.'

'About right for You-know-who's trip. Any collator sighting of You-know-who or Favard up in those parts?'

'Nothing. They could have been in and out very fast. It's remote. Didn't the girl say they were chortling over how surprisingly easy it was? They'd probably thought they'd have to hang about casing, waiting their chance.'

'But his heavies were off somewhere sulking at not landing their proper cut, if the nark's got it right.'

'And apparently his bird walked out on him a few weeks ago, so he'd be alone there.'

'Ideal.'

'Is this going to be an official entry at Dandy's?' Garland asked.

'I don't think so. Just a little look around. Imagine all the explaining to Iles. And he'd want a battalion there, as usual. Let's do it later tonight.' Harpur had sounded decisive but really was stiff with doubts. At that time he had considered it a distraction from the search for Street. He found out otherwise.

Now, he heard a car and went out to meet the Chief. It was April, but Lane had on a green-hooded Swedish military top-coat, meant for other ranks in the Arctic. As part of his policy of looking gritty, he went in a lot for army surplus. They walked to the outhouse. Garland, seated on some stinking sacks, was gazing at the bodies. One flashlight seemed exhausted and the other had begun to fade.

Street lay near the door, face towards it. His right hand held a Walther pistol. Lorraine was further into the outhouse also facing the door. Near him on the floor Harpur saw a large, silenced hand-gun, perhaps a Colt. In his brisk, know-all voice, Garland said: 'Our boy's been shot in the back of the head. Dandy in the chest. One bullet only, in each case. Pretty capable shooting, even so close. It doesn't look to me as if Ray Street was killed here.'

'My God, you can hardly see,' Lane replied. 'How have you decided that?'

'Not enough mess, sir. This is a point-blank head shot with a big-calibre bullet. I'd be looking for cranial fragments on the floor.'

The second flashlight yellowed, flickered, then went out. They stayed motionless for fear of falling over the bodies and talked in the dark.

Lane asked: 'Was our boy – Street you say he's called – was he assigned to watching Lorraine? I understood the target was Jamieson.'

'Correct, sir,' Harpur replied.

'So what's the link?'

'We think You-know-who may have been stalking Dandy, sir, because of a stolen load. You may remember an apparent hit-and-run where an airline man was injured. Street had been able to infiltrate Jamieson's operation, as you're aware.'

'And went out on a hit mission with him? Jesus Christ,

Harpur.'

'No, as a matter of fact, we're sure he didn't go, sir.'

'How are we sure? I don't like the look of this one bit.'

They heard more cars come up the dirt-track and slivers of the headlight beams occasionally flashed into the outhouse, passing swiftly over the faces of living and dead, like someone doing an inventory. When the engines stopped, Harpur shouted: 'In here. We're playing sardines. Tread carefully.'

Men appeared with more flashlights and began to set up proper lamps to run off the house electricity.

'Do we know whether the Walther belonged to Street?' Lane asked. 'Is that an issue weapon? Was he entitled to carry it?'

'It wouldn't be his, sir,' Garland replied. 'It's been put in his hand, if you ask me.'

'But that's sheer speculation?' the Chief said.

'At the moment, sir.'

'You've searched them?' Harpur asked.

'Nothing on either,' Garland replied.

'No warrant card?' Lane asked.

'No, sir.'

'Would Street carry it on this sort of job?' the Chief said.

'He's certainly under instructions to have it with him at all times,' Harpur replied.

'Not what I asked.'

'Yes, he would carry it,' Harpur said. Naturally Street never did when undercover. Making notes was bad enough.

Another car sped up to the house and in a moment Iles put his head around the door. For a few seconds he went and crouched over the body of Street and Harpur thought he might be weeping, his head turned to the shadows. 'This is down to that sod You-know-who, no question.'

'That's what I thought, sir,' Harpur said.

'How the hell do you work that out?' Lane demanded. 'Why couldn't it have been a straight shoot-out between these two, as it looks: our man hit first in the back of the head, but able to turn and kill Lorraine?'

Iles straightened, stared at the Chief for a couple of seconds and then ignored his question. 'We'll get him this time if I have to – ' He glanced towards the men fixing the lights and did not finish the threat, whatever it was.

The four of them went outside. 'Our boy has been dumped there, of course,' Iles said. 'Very artistic tableau. Not quite up to *Hamlet*.'

'Killed where, then?' Lane asked.

'At You-know-who's place, I should think,' Harpur replied. That bloody Chinese mat had to come up.

'They'd found out who he was?' Lane said.

'Has to be that,' Iles replied. 'I looked at his nostrils. That lad's been coking. Christ knows what he might have gabbled. It was always a danger we recognized.'

Rain thudded on the lined hood of the Swedish coat as they stood in front of the house's portico, watching the search of the rooms start.

Garland said: 'Obviously, two visits here by You-know-who and Favard, once to do Dandy, and then to bring Street and make it look like his job. All this rain, there won't be tracks, but that's how it must have been.'

'Agreed,' Iles said.

The Chief muttered: 'God, we're never going to find evidence that will stand up in court.'

Iles spun around and seemed for a moment about to scream into the hood around Lane's face. He pushed his own face hard against the opening but then drew back a little. 'We make sure we do have the evidence,' he snarled. 'We do whatever is necessary to provide it. We are talking about the death of a police officer here, sir. He's been murdered, knocked over from the back. We've had similar things before, and we always get the fucker who did it, somehow or other. Always. This is a kid of twenty-two who's done all sorts of great work for us, and that takes in catamiting himself to a known suck, and we see him right. We put You-know-who in court and make sure the jury get the full message, even if we have to do a little improvising. How would you like someone of yours flung into a shack with a piece of sludge like Dandy Lorraine, sir?'

Possibly Lane had never seen Iles at full frenzy before. The

Chief shifted inside his stout coat and said: 'Well, Desmond, Colin, if your readings are right, I hope we can do it.'

'Look at this blasted place,' Iles replied. 'The house has probably got quite a decent history behind it. I mean, it's not Blenheim Palace, but the lines are honest enough. There'd be a time when this whole thing – house, cottages, barns, outbuildings, farm – would be a fine unit of the landscape. Who's here now? What's here now? It's turned into a dark battleground for snow-runners and a down-grade vault for one of our brightest colleagues. We'll put it right. Who else will?'

When Lane had left and Garland was back in the outhouse, Iles and Harpur walked down to the lake. The rain was easing and once in a while the moon came clear of the clouds and gave some light.

'I don't think Lane is a total cunt, not at all,' Iles remarked. 'Never have and anyone who says otherwise is a liar. Poor dab is feeling his way, but one can't be too easy with him. He's got bags of genuine bottle there and in time he's going to be fine. I'm perfectly ready to help him. All the same, I think of the old Chief. Barton was ancient and very tired and very retarded but he had the most polished sense of loyalty I've ever met. We live by that, Col.'

'I thought it sharp of you to appeal to Mr Lane's sense of family.'

'Well, it sounded to me, I could be wrong, but it did seem that the sad idiot wanted to play fair on this one. That drool about evidence. It nauseated me for a bit, but I'm OK now.'

'Here's the dawn, almost,' Harpur said.

'You ought to get down to You-know-who's place right away. Turn them over a bit.'

'Yes, I'd thought of that.'

Iles gazed fondly as a moorhen laboriously made its way across the lake. 'Look, I'm sorry I wasn't around when you called. We might have been able to get things going without letting Lane in so early. It's done now, though. I was at Celia's when you rang, but you would have guessed that. Thanks for not interrupting there. We've something very satisfying going. I'd say it was as close to the real item as can be.'

'Nice.'

'I mustn't lose her, mustn't ever lose her.'

'Why should you, sir?'

Iles seemed to be quoting: 'Let us prove, while we can, the sports of love. You know it, Col? From *Volpone*. "Come, my Celia – ".'

'Well, I hope so.'

'Important I should find somebody, Col. I had a fear of being driven towards girl kids.'

'You've made a wise choice, sir.'

'She hated me at the start, naturally. People often do. It's all the radiant aplomb. I wish to God I could shred it and become diffident and meek. If Christ managed it, why can't I? Others like me first, then hate me. They think they've seen through me. Seen through? Damn all there, anyway. She's very responsive for the moment. I can see their needs, you know. They're always surprised at the way I can be car – '

He seemed about to say caring, but must have remembered this was a bloody Gerald Kaufman word and paused.

'The way I can be careful with their susceptibilities. It's really only a matter of sensitivity, but that's a rare attribute, I fear, these days.'

'Fine quality.'

'Been with me since a child. My mother always used to say she'd never known anyone so capable of sympathy and fellow feeling. At one time I thought it rather soft. No. Really, it's the basis of life. Yes.' He nodded several times. 'Right then, do we bring You-know-who and Favard in at once and knock seven different sorts of shit out of them?'

'In due course, I think, sir. I'll visit now, but we need to go carefully.'

'I meant, in view of the Chief's obvious wish to move fast and get unshakeable evidence.'

'I don't think we're quite ready.'

'Col, I realize you may be sitting on all sorts you haven't disclosed to me, as is your little way. You mess this up, you let Jamieson off the hook, and you're dead for keeps, you understand that? We don't forgive and we don't fuck up in a case like this. Don't mess me about, Harpur. If we're short of anything, get it. You understand? Get whatever we need to nail him. Get it somehow or another. I'll deal with Lane if there are any problems.' Fondly he gazed back at the lake, its surface occasionally ruffled by a squall. 'Gentleness above all is what I can offer women. Celia has had so little of that, the dear thing.'

Garland came from the outhouse and leaned against a wall, at the edge of a patch of light from one of the lamps, obviously craving fresh air.

'He's not so bad,' Iles remarked. 'When one is deep into a love relationship oneself one can forgive others for straying, Col, even one's wife. Well, I don't need to tell you, do I? It humanizes one, educates one. Yet, I'll never understand what that dull little creature, Sarah, saw in a lout like Garland.'

'Yes, I've heard before that an affair brings out the general sweetness in people.'

11

'Mr Harpur, may we now come to the matter of the tasselled and inscribed silver pencil which you said during your evidence in chief was found in the outhouse?'

'Yes, sir,'

'So that my lord and the jury may be absolutely clear, could you indicate to us on the photograph of the outhouse interior exactly where the silver pencil lay?'

'To the left of Raymond Street in a corner. Here.' He pointed.

'Several feet from the body?'

'Yes.'

'It was not hidden in any way by the body or clothes?'

'No, but it was obscured by some sacks of fertilizer kept there. It had rolled under the edge of one.'

'So, it was not in full view?'

'No, sir.'

'You have told the court that it was you, personally, who found the pencil.'

'That is correct.'

'I'd like to be precise on exactly when this was. Can you help me?'

'On my second visit to the outhouse.'

'When would that be?'

'At about 8 a.m. on 5th April last year.'

'Did you pick up the pencil?'

'Yes, sir.'

'Had the outhouse already been searched by others?'

'We had made a rough search when we discovered the bodies several hours earlier. But no properly organized search had been carried out at this time. It was due to take place later that morning when all the equipment arrived.'

'I see. Why was it necessary for you to go back to the outhouse?'

'It's something a detective does. One is always hoping to spot some item that's been missed.'

'And, of course, you saw that the pencil had initials inscribed on it – CCJ: Clifford Charles Jamieson?'

'I think I did see there was an inscription. The light was not perfect, even with the lamps. I don't believe I made out the letters until later.'

'If you please. What did you do with the pencil?'

'I put it in my pocket.'

'Did you show it to anyone?'

'Immediately?'

'Yes.'

'No, I was alone. Later, of course, I showed it to others and handed it to the exhibits officer.'

'Perhaps we can come to those matters in due course. I believe you said in your evidence in chief that during the night, when the bodies were found, Inspector Garland entered the outhouse first?'

'Yes.'

'It was dark, of course, but he was carrying a flashlight, was he not?'

'Yes.'

'Am I correct in thinking that later there was another flash-light and then a whole battery of lamps?'

'Yes.'

'Yet it was you, on a second visit, who saw the pencil on the floor and picked it up. Doesn't that seem odd to you? It wasn't in full view, but presumably it could be seen easily enough, or it wouldn't have been spotted by you.'

'There were other things to preoccupy Garland – two bodies, including one of a colleague.'

'We can ask Inspector Garland about that himself a little later. But the bodies must have preoccupied you, as well. I understand they were still there on your second visit. Is that correct?'

'Yes, they did, naturally. But the original shock had gone and I had time to look around.'

'And what you're telling us is that when you did have a chance to look around the first thing you saw was one of the major pieces of evidence in this trial – the silver pencil of my client, conveniently and incontrovertibly identified. That is so, isn't it?'

'I haven't said it was the first.'

'If you please. Can we say it was one of the first?'

'Yes.'

'Thank you. You must have felt unable to believe your luck.'

'Sir?'

'To come upon what you would obviously regard as a crucial piece of evidence at once.'

'My feelings at that time were overwhelmingly to do with the death of a fellow officer.'

'I see. Mr Harpur, the prosecution are making a great deal of this pencil, are they not?'

'It is part of the evidence.'

'You and my learned friend would like us to believe that it links my client with the death of Detective Constable Street?'

'It is part of the evidence.'

'Come now, detective chief superintendent, it is much,

much more than just another part, isn't it? Is it not the linchpin of the case, essential if you are to hold together your claim that the body of Street was brought from his home by my client and Paul Favard and dumped in the outhouse? You allege – wrongly allege – that this pencil fell from Mr Jamieson's pocket while he was helping place the body, do you not?'

'We regard the pencil as an important part of the evidence.'

'You see, what puzzles me, Mr Harpur, and what might well puzzle the jury is why you should have been the only one to have spotted the pencil. Can you enlighten us on that?'

'I thought I had explained. I was the only one present at the time of this second search.'

'If – as you wrongly suggest – my client had been there with a colleague and had dropped the pencil accidentally, don't you think he would have spotted it before leaving?'

'It was not easy to see. It could have been dark. They might well have been in a rush.'

'Mr Harpur, would it surprise you to know that my client never carried this pencil?'

'It would not surprise me to know that he says he never carried it.'

'Would it also surprise you to know that he always kept the pencil at home, among other items of sentimental value, it having been given him by his former wife, Kate?'

'It would not surprise me to know that he says he kept it at home.'

'Did you carry out searches at Mr Jamieson's home, Nightingale House, both before and immediately after the discovery of the bodies at the Lorraine farm?'

'Yes.'

'You had, in fact, been to Mr Jamieson's house in the early hours after discovery of the bodies, arriving at about 5.30 a.m. Although you had no warrant, you insisted on looking through the house. Is that correct?'

'Yes.'

'Am I right in saying that this would be the second time you had searched the house without a warrant?'

'Yes. Mr Jamieson did not object on either occasion.'

'Was he pleased to see you at 5.30 a.m.?'

'He was not pleased, but he did not object to the search. He seemed to regard it as a normal part of his life.'

'I see. The police hound him, is that what you mean?'

'We have had reason to call on him now and then.'

'Did he accompany you while you searched?'

'No.'

'On either occasion?'

'No.'

'He did not behave like someone who had things to hide, then?'

'He did not accompany me.'

'Tell me, Mr Harpur, in your various searches did you ever see this pencil in Nightingale House?'

'No.'

'Now, I'm sure your searches would be thorough, chief superintendent. You are a very experienced officer. Did you go into one of the small front bedrooms, the one with red flock wallpaper?'

'I went into every room.'

'On each search?'

'Yes.'

'Did you see an antique brass inkstand there?'

'Yes.'

'Did you look at it closely?'

'I examined it.'

'Yes, it is handsome – also a gift to Mr Jamieson, but from his mother. Did you during these examinations see the silver pencil lying on the inkstand?'

'No.'

'You're certain?'

'Yes.'

'How can you be so sure? Did you make notes?'

'No, sir.'

'Very well. Your aim, as I understand it, on each occasion, was to find any trace of Detective Constable Street. An inkstand, a silver pencil would be of passing interest, surely? Are you really certain the pencil was not there?'

'Yes, sir. I'd remember. It is a distinctive piece.'

'I'm going to suggest to you that it was on the inkstand, probably on both occasions when you searched.'

'No, sir.'

'I wish the jury to understand exactly what I'm saying, Mr Harpur: I put it to you that on one of those unsupervised visits, most likely the second, you picked up that pencil and took it secretly from the house, having noted it on the first visit and realized its potential usefulness as an exhibit?'

'No, sir.'

'Nobody was watching what you did. It would have been easy to take, would it not?'

'I suppose so. I haven't thought about it.'

'I suggest that you took it with the sole purpose of implicating my client in the deaths of Arnold Lorraine and Raymond Street by saying that it was found in the outhouse.'

'That is not true. It is a disgraceful suggestion.'

'It would certainly be a disgraceful act, would it not, chief superintendent?'

'Entirely. Unthinkable.'

'We at least have agreement on that. I am suggesting that your motives were in a way understandable, but very wrong. For you, this is an important case, is it not?'

'Yes. Two people were killed by firearms, one a police officer.'

'Exactly: one a police officer. I don't think I exaggerate when I say there is exceptional loyalty among police officers. That is so?'

'We support each other within the law.'

'If you please. Would it be true to say that when a police officer is murdered quite exceptional efforts are made to find the killer?'

'Considerable efforts are made to find any murderer, sir.'

'Quite so. But the killing of a policeman – that is regarded as an attack on the whole Force, isn't it? Like an assault upon all police officers? He is part of you. Isn't that so?'

'Street was a colleague.'

'A very young and talented colleague?'

'Yes.'

'And this young man had been snuffed out in a particularly dastardly way from behind, hadn't he?'

'Yes.'

'Chief superintendent, you want to avenge that, don't you?'

'I'm not in the vengeance business, sir. I wish to see his murderer convicted, as I would wish to see any murderer convicted.'

'But I thought we had already decided this was not just any murderer, hadn't we?'

'Sir, you had decided it.'

'Mr Harpur, who was responsible for putting Detective Constable Street to watch Mr Jamieson?'

'Street was one of my men.'

'So the answer must be that you were responsible?'

'Yes.'

'Nobody else?'

'I chose him.'

'During this kind of work he would be very closely involved with the officer directing the operation, wouldn't he? There would be a particularly interdependent relationship between an undercover man and his superior, wouldn't there?'

'Street was under my control.'

'So that naturally, in such circumstances, his death would weigh very heavily on you, wouldn't it?'

'It does.'

'Perhaps – and please correct me if I am misrepresenting you – perhaps weigh more on you than the death of someone for whom you had no responsibility, such as Arnold Lorraine? Is that so?'

'That would be natural.'

'Perfectly so. I'm not trying to trap you, chief superintendent. I'm glad we can reach another point of agreement. Now, if you suspected – genuinely though mistakenly suspected – that my client was somehow implicated in Raymond Street's death, you would be determined to bring him to justice, wouldn't you?'

'Yes.'

'After all, that is your job, isn't it?'

'Yes.'

'But more than the demands of the job, you would feel some personal blame for what had happened – as you've indicated. Is that not so?'

'Blame is not the word. It was my duty to order someone to this assignment. If it hadn't been Street it would have been someone else. I realize that because of my choice he is dead. That distresses me.'

'Of course, of course. What I am putting to you, Mr Harpur, is that the exceptional, tragic aspect of this death, and your own involvement in it, led you to behave in a fashion which, I'm sure, is also exceptional and totally out of keeping with the way you normally conduct your duties.'

'I don't think I follow.'

'I have to suggest that your determination to see the killer of Detective Constable Street punished led you to fabricate a crucial piece of evidence.'

'That is rubbish.'

'You feared, and rightly feared, that there would be inadequate authentic evidence to convict my client. How could there be adequate evidence, when he had no part in this dastardly affair? I suggest that the intense feeling of loyalty to one of your men, and your belief that you were somehow responsible for the death, led you to take the tasselled pencil from the inkstand, knowing it could be used to implicate Clifford Jamieson.'

'No, sir.'

'The pencil was not on the floor of the outhouse at all when you arrived for your second search, after the visit to Nightingale House, was it?'

'Yes, sir.'

'I have to suggest that you simply reported having found it there, and that you went there on this second visit so that you could pretend to have found the pencil then.'

'I found it where I said, sir.'

'Mr Harpur, on occasions like this – the murder of a gifted young police officer – the man in charge of the case can come under very powerful pressure from his superiors to secure an arrest and conviction. Did that happen to you?'

'No, sir. Everyone of all ranks wanted the case cleared up, of course. But no undue pressure was applied by any of the officers above me.'

'Come now, chief superintendent, are you really saying that at no stage were you told that it was desperately important to make an arrest and bring someone to trial?'

'There would have been no need to tell me that, sir. I knew it and felt it for myself.

'In some ways I'm quite fond of him, Col,' Iles declared, chuckling delightedly. 'He's got the kilograms and the flabby chops, and one of their wigs does need a porker face under it if it's not to resemble shagged-out streamers on a maypole. Let me have men about me that are gross. By comparison, our brief looks pretty dirty minded and ulcered, don't you think? And old blubber cheeks, Larnog QC, has all that wonderful, mouldy Lincoln's Inn vocab – "dastardly", "linchpin", "I don't believe I exaggerate". Atavistic flourishes like that come dear. Larnog's going to cost You-know-who a fair few dozen grand. But he's made a wise selection. That tub is making quite a defence. I wonder how Jamieson picked him. Larnog must be queer, I suppose. Ghastly to imagine him at it. The jaw's very prominent. Gays look after each other in exemplary fashion, almost up to my lot in the Brotherhood. Queer Masons, now: they'd be the giddy ultimate in *esprit de corps*.

'Larnog knows Jamieson killed our boy, of course, Col, knows it as well as we do – and that he killed all the rest. But he'll still do his turn like a trouper. Bags of vim and dexterity inside that Oliver Hardy suit. Sometimes I do wonder if the silver pencil was a bit much. It's the initials naturally, that take it that little bit over the top. Too much of a clincher. What does my fat, learned friend say? Where's the transcript? Yes: "conveniently and incontrovertibly identified." True one has to hit a British jury bloody hard and with everything that's available and a bit more besides, if possible, or they'll always find some dodge to sell the police short. This whole lot look as perverse and Trot as any I've ever seen. What do they care that a kid's been polluted and slaughtered trying to keep drugs off the streets so their own kids will be safe from the habit? They think it should all be done in talks by teachers and the occasional anti-junky ad on telly. Do they know what we're fighting? Do they care? Do they, balls. Mind you, they're not going to know that our boy had to turn himself into a suck for the sake of good policing. That lot, they'd probably think he enjoyed it. A couple of them could be customers of You-know-who. Noticed the eyes of the little bony cow in the front row next to the foreman? She takes something tastier than snuff. Hard to know whether they'll swallow the pencil. When they take a look at You-know-who they're going to ask whether someone with a phiz like that can write. A couple of them had a right smirk when Larnog was doing his piece about how sweetly lucky you'd been to find something so conclusive right at the start. But I'm not blaming you, Col. The pencil did seem a good idea. We both saw the risks of overplaying. Our brief did bloody well with it, too, even if he does look like a day in the life of a gusset. I could see Jamieson thinking about leg irons when you were doing your evidence in chief.'

They were talking in Iles's house. Harpur heard Sarah moving about upstairs. Iles paused, also listening. 'She's found out about Celia and me. Says I'd better go. I think she's right. It will cause a bit of a stir, I suppose. Assistant Chiefs aren't supposed to shack up with drug-runners' molls. These funny old prejudices linger on.'

'You've got to follow your heart, sir.'

'Wonderful organ. Entitles one to knock hell out of all the rules and promises, doesn't it? On the whole, I'm in favour, despite my frosty, righteous appearance and the heavy Prot upbringing.'

'When, sir?'

'What?'

'When do you expect to move out?'

'Not too long. It's tough here now.' Iles winced. 'Yes you were fine with your evidence and good standing up to Larnog,

I thought. All I'd add, Col, is don't push so hard, you dim twat. When you said it was disgraceful to suggest you would plant evidence, just said it as if it was the first, inevitable word that had sprung from your affronted soul, it came over damn well, sounding hurt and heartfelt. But then, you stupid prat, you had to add "unthinkable". Too big a notion. Of course it's bloody well thinkable, and everyone in court knew it, from the screws up. By granting yourself that flutter of indignation you made them all consider the opposite of what you'd said. Rhetoric's a deep art and you haven't got the mind for it. Keep things simple and mild. I know nobody better at that than you, Col, and it's a golden privilege to work with you, and to have the chance of these little talks at the end of the day.' The front door slammed as Sarah went out. 'I suppose she's got something going herself,' Iles said. 'She took ages to get over your friend, Garland. Has he re-activated the relationship? Not that I'd be bothered now.'

'I'd feel a lot happier if we could call Jill Younger as part of our case, sir,' Harpur replied.

'Not on, absolutely not, Col. I've told you and Lane has told you. Nothing has changed.'

'She's the only one who can say Street was in You-know-who's place and alive an hour before the medics fix death.'

'I've heard the arguments and I've read reports of what she might testify. We do without her. I don't even want to meet or see her. Our case doesn't need the helping of a snorting slag. Christ, Harpur, people and juries already think we're horse shit. How's it going to look if we bring in a piece of galloping pussy saying she was Street's bed-mate? We're portraying him as a clever, wholesome youth, blotted out before his time by a villain.'

The room they were in was magnificently furnished with tasteful and comfortable modern chairs, settees and a fine, low sideboard. Dust lay thick on this and on most other surfaces in the room, and what looked like discarded crisp packets and pages of newspaper had been rolled together and pushed into a corner behind the video-player. Sarah must be very preoccupied with something outside the house.

'Who's likely to believe a creature like the Younger girl if she goes in to the box, anyway, Col? And what's her evidence going to be – that she and Street were coking and poking all over Nightingale House, including in You-know-who's own bedroom, smashing a revered picture of the venerable Mrs Jamieson in their hot cavortings? Such a lovely image of a police officer. Then, if the fat lad is really battering her with questions and trying to piss on her story, she's liable to retaliate and let it out to him and the world that she's sure Jamieson killed Street, not because his cover had gone, but because Ray was his lady-love and he didn't like his lady-loves having lady-loves of their own and especially not in the same bed. What kind of nobility and stature would be left to Street then, or to any of us? What sort of Force are we supposed to be running here? Boys for sale? We consign a kid to dong-diving? Do you see Lane or me or you going any further if that lot spilled? The only thin blue line that would matter for us would be drawn under our careers. Christ, I'm already due for a load of very nasty trouble when the Celia Mars business becomes known. Of course, none of this career stuff matters a fish's tit. I want to make that totally clear. What matters is how people see this lad of ours. Street was a skilled and dedicated officer and he was murdered because his cover went wrong somehow. We stick to that. We don't know how he was rumbled. It's not important. That was the motive, not some putrescent pansy spat that went too far. Street was murdered for doing his duty, not for doing a floozy. That's our case.'

'But – '

'I see your point, Col, and I respect it fully. Certainly it deserves consideration, which has been given, so now kindly drop it for fucking keeps, would you? Can you really see the Mick allowing Jill Younger's story to get loose? Jesus, Lane thinks all single Catholic WPCs are virgins. For all I know, he may believe it of the men as well. Get away now, Col, to your bit of consolation if she's still available. You deserve it. You're putting up a brilliant show in there, and Garland will do even better when it's his turn. That one could fool the recording angel.'

'Mr Harpur, I would now like to look in a little more detail, if I may, at the searches conducted by you and other officers at Nightingale House. When did you first search this property?'

'I visited the house a few days before the bodies of Street and Lorraine were found. I wouldn't describe it as a search.'

'But you told us you went into every room. Does that not constitute a search?'

'I –'

'What you mean is you didn't turn it over, isn't it?'

'It was a visit.'

'What were you looking for?'

'Anything to indicate that Street had been in the house recently.'

'Did you find any such indication?'

'Not on that first visit.'

'Mr Harpur, please: we are discussing only that first visit at present. Would you answer the question yes or no, please?'

'No. I did not find anything.'

'May we now come to the second visit, the one in the early hours of 5th April? Was there any reason why this call should have been made so early?'

'The bodies were discovered during the night and we were working around the clock at this stage. It just happened that our visit to Nightingale House fell at that time.'

'Come now, chief superintendent, is it not an established police tactic to disrupt households in the small hours, when people are at their least resistant?'

'It was a simple time-tabling matter.'

'Was my client the first person you called on?'

'I think so.'

'Was he?'

'Yes.'

'Why?'

'Because Street had been working for him.'

'You had absolutely no firm evidence to connect Street with the house, had you?'

104

'I have said, he was working for Mr Jamieson. It seemed a natural place to start inquiries.'

'Very well. Were you determined to harass and bully my client while he was still half asleep?'

'The visit had to be made when officers were available.'

'Yes, you were not alone this time, were you? How many officers were present? I don't think this was brought out in your earlier evidence.'

'Perhaps a dozen.'

'Perhaps? Can't you do better than that?'

'Fourteen.'

'Plus dogs?'

'Yes.'

'Sniffer dogs?'

'Yes. We suspected there might be drugs on the premises.'

'Did those highly trained animals find anything?'

'No, sir.'

'In your various searches have any drugs ever been found at Nightingale House?'

'No.'

'Mr Harpur, when the prosecution looked about for a motive in these killings they decided on drug trafficking. Their case – indeed, of course, your case, the police case – is that my client is involved in that business, and that the killings arise from some sort of feud between dealers. Is there any piece of tangible evidence to link my client with drug trafficking?'

'Well, sir – '

'Please answer. Is there?'

'No drugs have been found.'

'Thank you very much. Now, if we may return to the search of the house after the bodies had been discovered: you were looking once more for any trace that Raymond Street had been in the property recently. This was your prime objective, was it not?'

'Yes. We suspected that he might have been killed there.'

'Why did you suspect that?'

'It seemed to us on a first examination that he had not been killed in the outhouse.'

'Yes, I understand that. But what is the step of reasoning which says that because he might not have been killed in the outhouse he must have been killed at Mr Jamieson's home?'

'It seemed a possibility.'

'You had no evidence for this?'

'We were looking for evidence.'

'Could we get this clear, please? You had absolutely nothing to suggest a link between Street and Nightingale House, but you and a posse of officers with dogs went there at dawn looking for such a connection. Does that strike you as proper and reasonable police behaviour?'

'We were acting at speed, sir.'

'Mr Harpur, is it true that you gave orders that the men with you should concentrate on the downstairs rooms while you looked at the bedrooms?'

'At the start, yes.'

'Why?'

'Downstairs rooms are generally more difficult to search. There tend to be more articles and more furniture. The main body of men would be needed there.'

'While you went alone upstairs?'

'At the beginning I was alone, yes. They came up and helped afterwards.'

'And, to go back over ground already covered, it was while you were alone that you went into the bedroom containing the antique inkstand?'

'Yes.'

'No officer need have seen you pick up the pencil?'

'It was not there.'

'I think you said earlier that on neither search did Mr Jamieson accompany you. On both occasions, then, you would have been totally unobserved? Is that so?'

'Yes.'

'Now, we have heard you say in your main evidence that when some of the other men came upstairs you and they lifted a Chinese carpet in the main bedroom, the one where Mr Jamieson had been sleeping until your arrival. You seemed very determined to get this carpet up. Had you seen it before?'

'Yes.'

'Had you some special reason for thinking Detective Constable Street had been in this room?'

'Lifting the carpet was a part of the search. We moved many pieces of furniture and other floor coverings.'

'If you please. Now, you told my learned friend that on removing the carpet you found certain floor boards which appeared to you to have been recently re-planed and re-sanded. My lord and the jury have visited the room and you indicated the boards in question. Mr. Harpur, it was necessary for you to indicate them, was it not, because no great difference was apparent between those boards and the rest?'

'Certain differences.'

'What?'

'Plane markings.'

'But there were plane markings on many of the boards. That sometimes happens during preparation for sanding, doesn't it?'

'On the boards in question the marks were more obvious.'

'Well, the jury will decide about that. Now, you have told my learned friend that you were interested in those boards because you think Detective Constable Street was shot in this room and that his blood fell on the floor and stained it before the carpet had been bought and put down. That is so?'

'Yes.'

'On what grounds did you believe that?'

'It was one of a number of options we considered.'

'Very well. How did you arrive at these options?'

'We had to give thought to every possibility.'

'Mr Harpur, we are not making any progress, are we? We'll move on. Scientific tests have not discovered any traces of blood on the boards, have they?'

'I understand that the kind of deep planing we are talking about would remove them.'

'What we have here, chief superintendent, is the allegation that a man was murdered in this bedroom based on the fact – the alleged and disputed fact – that a few parts of the floor appear to have been recently re-treated. That is the whole strength of it, is it not?'

'No, the carpet itself is significant.'

'Oh, are you saying now that the carpet itself showed blood-stains?'

'No, but it was the only room where a full-sized carpet had been laid. It was a recent purchase.'

'I see. Because my client chooses to bring a certain extra comfort to his bedroom you thought he must be concerned to hide something?'

'I considered that might be so.'

'By buying a carpet he laid himself open to suspicion of murder? Is that what you're saying?'

'It was unusual for the style of the house.'

'Mr Harpur, are you really asking the jury to take this seriously? Isn't it nonsense?'

'No, sir.'

'When you get out of bed in the morning don't you like to put your feet on to a carpet, rather than cold boards? Isn't it conceivable that Mr Jamieson might feel the same?'

'The carpet was out of keeping.'

'I have to put it to you, Mr Harpur, that you went to Nightingale House on 5th April with the fixed intention of discovering something, anything, that would link my client with these deaths.'

'I went to carry out a search.'

'You were under severe pressure to arrest someone for the murder of Detective Constable Street, and, incidentally, the murder of Arnold Lorraine. That is so, isn't it?'

'I wished to apprehend the killer or killers.'

'You feared, and very rightly, that your dogs and the rest of the search party would come up with absolutely nothing, didn't you, and so the total burden fell on you to produce something, to produce anything, didn't it?'

'I was part of a search team.'

'In charge of that team. You saw some opportunity to make a point from the purchase of the carpet, and you persisted with that, didn't you?'

'I looked for evidence.'

'Why did you choose the bedrooms for your share of the search? You were in charge and could have taken any section of the house.'

'It happened that way.'

'You had no evidence to draw you especially to the master bedroom, had you?'

'I took each in turn.'

'Christ, Harpur, that carpet stuff and the floor-boards saga – so feeble,' Iles said.

'It was all true, sir.'

Iles turned in his seat and stared at him. 'What's true is what a jury believes. That material sounded like something from a tired, desperate mind. We could lose everything we gained with the silver pencil. This cop-killer and kid-killer might dodge out again.'

Harpur was driving him to see Simon Wood at his smart house on the cliffs.

'Col, you'll say we could have nailed him if Jill Younger gave evidence and testified she left Street in the bed. That's your view, a strong one, but forget it. Wood's our last hope. He'll look good in the box, almost fit but with enough signs from the hit-and-run to get sympathy.'

'How's Celia, sir?'

'She still speaks of him. There's a certain *tendresse*.'

'And does it go?'

'All I ever wanted in a woman. You know, I'd more or less given up sex as a bad job. I was taking a very anti line on the whole thing. So wrong, so sad and wrong. She's shown me that. I don't think I could manage without her now.'

They parked and knocked on Wood's smart red front door. From a few miles out in the darkness a fog-horn sounded. 'Ah, Simon, grand,' Iles said, 'you're looking fine. Who'd have thought ten months ago at the hospital you'd be rampaging about the way you are now?'

'I'm damn glad you came,' Wood replied. 'Cold feet have been setting in. I hate the thought of going into the box.'

'Nothing to bother about, believe me,' Iles told him. 'Larnog's a piece of greasy antiquity, a mountainous ninny, more like the Albert Hall than Marshall-Hall. Quite a room this. Glad you were able to put some by.'

It was a long, modern house with big windows to the sea and the islands. Wood lowered venetian blinds now. There was still the trace of a limp as he moved, but only a trace. He had one visible scar, about two inches long on his forehead over the right eye.

'Celia sends her very best,' Isles said. 'She may look in to the court tomorrow.'

'I'd rather she didn't, really.'

'It'll be your big day. Don't be so modest,' Iles replied. 'You're our star.'

They sat down in large, blue-upholstered armchairs and Wood put a bottle of rum and three glasses on an onyx table. They helped themselves.

'Sometimes I think I can't go through with it,' Wood muttered.

Iles gave him a good smile, full of understanding and comradeship. 'But of course you do, Simon. We understand that. It's to your credit. Giving evidence against former colleagues, as it were – bound to be a wrench. Only some congenital rat could do that without feeling self-reproach. The fact is, though, that while you're pissing about with your fine conscience and uncertainties, inside you know without a fragment of doubt that you've got to go through with it, isn't that so? A crook like you drowned conscience after kindergarten.'

Wood held up his hands. 'OK, OK, I know. If I don't do my piece you withdraw immunity and I'm sent away for running coke.'

'That's to put it very crudely, Simon,' Iles replied. 'You weren't made for Pentonville. Nice education, nice job, nice plump body that would get them smacking their dirty lips on the landings.'

'Don't look at You-know-who and Favard when you're in the box,' Harpur suggested. 'Face the jury. Don't panic. Rely on us. Jamieson and Favard are both going away for a long time after this. They're each charged with Street's murder and it will stick. They won't be able to give you trouble. You're very important to us, Simon – our strongest bit of evidence that trafficking took place.'

'You-know-who's got a lot of friends,' Wood said, 'and I'll be offending all sorts, not just him. I'm giving away the secrets of a very big industry.'

'We'll take care of you,' Iles said. 'Celia is sure you've got the bottle to do it. Very impressed by your courage, as a matter of fact. She still thinks highly of you. Irritating sometimes.'

'You and Celia are – ?'

'We discuss all sorts together, Celia and I. Beautiful swimmer, as you know, and full of laughter and French proverbs.'

'I used to miss her a hell of a lot.'

'I'm going to tell her. She'll be touched.'

'Simon, the cross-examination technique against people who turn Queen's evidence is to try to discredit them as witnesses,' Harpur said.

'Larnog will drag your character in the mire to make out you're untrustworthy,' Iles added. 'But you can cope. All you have to remember is that when it's over you walk out of the court free and nothing's going to hurt you, not us, not You-know-who. You can come back here and sit peacefully at your window, now and then crying out to the ships, "Whither away fair rover, What thy quest?"'

'I just give a totally factual account of the trafficking system, as I knew it, and the arrangement with Jamieson?'

'Exactly,' Iles replied. 'And details of your pay-off – the hard cash.'

Wood put a hand to the scar. 'Bloody hard.'

'We'd like to go over the circumstances of your accident again,' Harpur said.

'You parked the Volvo and walked with the brief-case towards Street and Favard in their Toyota,' Iles recited. 'After a few minutes you heard a fast moving vehicle behind you. All that is simple fact. Easy, isn't it? When you turn to see what's happening you are able to make out Dandy Lorraine, whom you know as a competing dealer, in the passenger seat. You had a bloody good look at him.'

'This is the bit that troubles me,' Wood replied. 'I think it was Dandy, but, of course, everything happened so fast, and it was dark.'

'But at the end the car was very close. It had no lights, so you weren't dazzled,' Iles told him. 'Simon, you saw Lorraine.'

'I certainly saw someone like him.'

'We've been over this before, Wood,' Iles remarked softly. 'Shall I spell it out yet again? You saw Lorraine. He was unmistakable – the moustache, the big nose, the mottled skin. You do understand, do you, that when we're up against someone who's guilty of all the things we know Jamieson to be guilty of we use everything to get him? You're part of the everything Wood – a big part. If we can't have him for Street's murder, or a few he did before that, we'll have him for Lorraine's. They all mean life. Your job is to tell the jury why he might want to do Dandy, savvy? Lorraine has run down one of his best boys, namely you, and picked up one of his juiciest packages. That's the motive, and you're the one to describe it. I'll tell you straight, Simon, Mr Harpur and I would like to see you go down for a long while, especially after you messed us about with wrong information on the vehicle that hit you. Remember that little fantasy? But there's a deal now with you, and we'll stick to it. I hope we know what honour and fidelity are. We admire you, Simon: your ability to pull through the way you have, your taste in women, these charming ebony figurines. We know perfectly well that we can depend on you.'

Wood said: 'Their lawyer's going to – '

'You balls this up and you'll be needing him yourself next,' Iles said. 'You'd have to sell this coastguard station to pay for his first day.'

12

Melanie Jill Younger learned about the acquittals of You-
know-who and Favard from local television news, and at first
could not believe what she heard. She gave a scream and sat
down quickly, head lowered and her hands over her ears.
When she looked back at the screen, film showed both men
beaming and accepting congratulations outside the court, and
she knew there had been no mistake. Someone was shaking a
champagne bottle as at the end of a Grand Prix, and You-
know-who had a glass in his hand.

He gave an interview. As he spoke, a smart, grey-haired
woman wearing a tweed coat, and introduced by the television
reporter as Mr Jamieson's mother, clutched his arm and
nodded fondly at all the points he made. She, too, held a champagne glass. Jill recognized her from the framed photograph
that Street had sent crashing in the big bedroom at Nightingale
House. Favard remained at the edge of the picture but turned
his back to the camera.

'Do you feel any bitterness towards the police as a result of
this case, Mr Jamieson?' the reporter asked.

'Not bitterness, but I am worried that two innocent people
can be treated the way we were just because police make
mistakes and bring charges. I know they got a job to do but
where the freedom of the individual is concerned they should
be more careful.'

'Would you consider action against the police?'

'That's something my lawyers will be talking about. I trust
them to do whatever is best. At the moment, all I can think is
gratitude to have this terrible thing lifted from my shoulders.'

'It's obvious, isn't it, that the jury did not believe the main
part of the police evidence and did not accept some of the prin-
cipal prosecution witnesses, such as Simon Wood?'

'We both want to say a very sincere thank-you to the jury.
When you think, they heard police officer after police officer

say awful things against us, yet they could still make up their own mind and find us innocent. This jury has proved that British justice is still something real and I say thank God for it.'

'But it wasn't only police evidence that was rejected. Do you think this case says anything about the use by police of informers with whom they've struck a deal?'

'Well, I don't know about that. I've heard about them supergrasses and so on in Belfast, but I never thought that sort of thing could happen to myself. It's like a terrible dream.'

'So, have you any idea at all how Detective Constable Street and Mr Lorraine met their deaths?'

'None whatsoever. How could I? I told the court that, and answered all them questions about the tragic deaths, and again the jury believed us. I would like to say that I greatly regret the death of a police officer, and I can understand why other police feel so strong about it. But that is no excuse for what happened to us – all the months in gaol, with this hanging over us.'

As she watched and listened, Jill Younger began to weep.

The camera moved in on You-know-who's mother. 'Mrs Jamieson, what are your feelings today?'

'Great relief, of course, and deep thankfulness to the good God that justice has been done.'

'Did you ever doubt that your son and Mr Favard would be found not guilty?'

'Never. Not for a moment. I knew they were innocent, and I knew God would not allow them to suffer further.' She stretched up and kissed You-know-who's cheek and he slipped an arm around her and squeezed her to him. 'I feel there should be a public inquiry into the way these police officers behaved, and I would like to see it carried out by some impartial body, not by the police themselves.'

'Will you and your son make an official demand for an inquiry?'

'We shall consult his lawyers, as he said. But it is certainly a possibility.'

'What are your plans now, Mr Jamieson?'

'Well, I hear a little celebration party is arranged across the road here in the Martyr, and we'll be going there. I think it might last quite a while. I want to say thank you to so many people, and especially to my lawyers, who had to deal with all those terrible things that were brought against us, and who have become my very good friends during all this trouble. And I will be meeting all the people who have stood by me, other friends and business colleagues, to say how grateful I am for their support. I don't believe I could have got through it all without them. Come to the party yourself – all the media. You'll be very welcome. And, then, afterwards, I'll go home, I expect, to see how my lovely house is. It's a long time since I've been there. I'm looking forward to sleeping in my own bed again.'

'In that now famous bedroom!'

'In that now famous bedroom, yes. Famous because it's got a bit of carpet on the boards. Who'd have thought it, though? Just be careful if you were thinking of going out and spending a bit on some floor covering, or you might have the heavy mob descending on you.'

'Thank you very much, Mr Jamieson.'

'Thank you.'

The camera watched You-know-who and his mother stroll away together, Favard and some other men carrying briefcases behind.

For a second, Jill Younger continued to cry, staring at the next news item, but still seeing what had just appeared. Then she suddenly dredged and spat hugely at the screen. The spittle hung and swung there as the weatherman came up, blurring part of his map and festooning his smile. Briefly, she opened her wallet and looked at the picture of Ray Street, the man she had known as Ray Milton. It had been a shock to find in the court reports that he was a cop, a big shock, but to her surprise her feelings for him never changed. She closed the wallet.

She had on a housecoat but now began to dress quickly in her red leather trousers and candy-striped blouse, then telephoned for a taxi. While waiting for it, she prepared a good snow snort and took it aboard with slow relish. When the car arrived she told the driver to get her to the Martyr fast.

115

She found the party still throbbing in the cocktail lounge. The crowd of hangers-on, relatives and lawyers seemed to have taken the place over, and she could understand why. Who would want to be in the same room as this loud crowd of filth and fellow-travellers? The room looked to her like all that was wrong with Britain. The scum was getting on top.

There were some yells and shouts about the trousers when she entered the bar; all the usual slime and insults. Most of the guests were far gone now, so you could forgive them if you felt like it, but she did not feel like it. They had turned the place into Sewersville, and that was how any place would be where this lot came together. Maybe they thought she was on the game tonight, and looking for business. This lot would think any girl was on the game at any time for the right cash.

Gravy-train lawyers made the place stink of sweat on top-class serge. 'Where's your shining patron?' she asked one of them.

'Only one among so many of us? Did they send out for you, doll?'

'No, it was you he sent out for, and a few others, and you all came running, hands grabbing for lolly. And you did a great job for him. You turned shit into champagne.'

From somewhere in his boozed frame the lawyer found a dose of dignity. 'We presented the truth, no more, no less.'

'Knock it off.'

She spotted You-know-who in a corner, talking with his mother and a man in a suit as big as a car cover, and made for them. 'You don't know me, You-know-who, but I know you,' she said.

'Parse that,' the fat man chuckled.

'Yes, I know you, love. From the decorators. Welcome. Have a drink. Here's my mother and Jeremy Larnog QC.'

'Fond of working for killers, then, Jerry?' she asked.

Larnog chuckled grandly again. 'I can see you're really full of very high-quality material, quite ready to fly.'

'You had it easy, you know that? I should have been there.'

'Yes?' Larnog replied. He beamed behind the cigar but she could see his eyes working hard as he tried to sort her out.

'Who is she, Clifford?' Mrs Jamieson demanded. 'What does she want? She should be turned out. Call the manager. This is intolerable.'

'Mummy, it's a party, a celebration. We mustn't have unpleasantness.'

'Know something, old piece?' Jill shouted. 'We knocked your bloody picture to smithereens, and I wish I could do it to you.'

Mrs Jamieson recoiled a step. 'Clifford, what does she mean?'

'I don't know what she means,' You-know-who replied. His voice had changed, the phoney friendship gone for the season. Suddenly, the noise in the bar fell as people tried to listen.

'Of course you know: darling mother's picture in your bed-room. The killing ground.'

'You're really having a go, aren't you?' Larnog muttered. 'You're police? Can you actually be police? You're badly hurt about this man, Street? A colleague? More than that?'

'I didn't even know Ray was police until this case. But, yes, I'm hurt. Christ, am I hurt? I got no time for police, but I did have time for Ray. And this one and Favard have done him. Don't tell me you didn't suss that, Jerry. That's not part of the job, is it, to make out a known killer's a saint? I know you sell a service, but I thought you had to believe in your client, even if it's only a fraction.'

'But she's vile,' Mrs Jamieson shrieked.

'At least you'll know there's been one decent man-and-woman screw in your poncy son's bed. It's not all laddy romps.'

'Oh, I cannot take this,' Mrs Jamieson cried.

'It's time for me to be away,' Larnog told You-know-who. 'Must get the last London train.'

'Have they got your address for the cheque, Jerry? You bet they have.'

Larnog leaned over to his side, like a great stricken building, and whispered: 'If I were you, I'd go myself now, little girl. Everyone's been pretty restrained, but I wouldn't push it.'

Favard approached. The noise in the bar had picked up

again, but was still nothing like what it had been earlier.

Jill said: 'When you get up there in your Inn of Court, or whatever, you can tell them what a great job you did getting these two bits of offal off, but if the bloody police had let me into the case, I could have made such a beautiful, beautiful mess of you. I could have made sure they paid for what they did to Ray. You really want them back on the streets, do you?'

'Harpur sent you down here to foul things up,' You-know-who snarled.

Favard suddenly took a grip on both her arms from behind and although she struggled and kicked he held her with ease.

Larnog seemed about to intervene. 'Oh, I don't think that's the way to deal with things, surely. She's in a state, that's all. For the moment her mind's blown. Little that she says is important. The thing is over and settled.' But he did nothing.

Mrs Jamieson did. She lunged at Jill's face with orange painted finger nails and Favard's hands tightened. 'You disgusting little foul-mouthed bitch,' Mrs Jamieson screamed, 'coming here with your lies and abuse to spoil everything.'

Jill felt her skin tear and screamed herself, kicking out now at the woman's legs.

Larnog yelled: 'No, no, please.'

Mrs Jamieson fell back again and sat down, holding her knee and weeping. You-know-who bent over her. He looked up and grunted at Favard: 'Keep tabs on the little piece, you hear?'

A man in a morning suit pushed his way towards Favard and Jill: 'I'm the deputy manager. I've called the police. Would you release the lady now, sir? Madam, are you hurt?' he asked Mrs Jamieson.

'What about me?' Jill howled. 'I'm in shreds.'

The deputy manager turned back to Favard. 'Sir, would you please release this lady now?'

Favard's hold slackened, and as soon as she felt free, Jill broke loose, stooped and spat in Mrs Jamieson's face. 'I've been practising,' she said.

13

The names of officers killed on duty were recorded on individual marble panels in the central hall at headquarters and, after the immediate distress of the death had passed, an unveiling ceremony for friends and relatives always took place. The tradition had been started decades ago, though there were comparatively few early entries. The number of new names had accelerated sharply in the last seven or eight years. People called this part of the building the Halo Wall.

It was almost twelve months after Street's killing before the ceremony for him, since Lane did not feel it would be appropriate until the trial finished. Street's mother, father and a sister came, and the Chief personally took them under his wing. To Harpur the parents looked astonishingly young – not much older than himself – and somehow that deepened the darkness. He would have liked to dodge out of the whole thing, but knew he couldn't. Above all, he wanted to be somewhere else when the curtains fell back and revealed Street's name and dates, 1963–1986. The span was so agonizingly short, like a war-cemetery inscription. As the crowd assembled, Harpur stood with Iles at the back of the hall.

'The Mick will do this impeccably, Col. He has a wonderful way with feelings and a rehearsed route to genuineness.' The ACC was in uniform and medals for the occasion, looking bonny and grand, grey but unstoppable. 'The family are gems. I went to see them straight after Street's death. They strengthened me, helped me get through my grief. This is not a fucking chaplain do, is it? No bloody Last Trump stuff and that what is man that thou art mindful malarkey?'

'Don't think so sir.'

'I'd rather mourn without the professionals.'

'Street wasn't a Mason, was he, sir?'

'What's that supposed to mean, you venomous ape? Are you saying I grieve about nobody but the Brotherhood?'

'OK, OK, Sir.'

'Well, are you?' he bellowed, shattering the churchy hush of the assembling congregation. People turned to stare and those who knew Iles soon resumed as before the outburst.

Lane brought Street's family down towards them. The Chief was in uniform, too, but still genial-looking and homely. Iles greeted them: 'Mr Street, Mrs Street, Angela, what can I say? We let them get away. I promised you and promised you they wouldn't. You must think so ill of us. Perhaps we can do something yet, though.'

'It doesn't seem to matter now,' Mrs Street replied. She was short, dark-haired and burly, in a sheepskin coat.

'Oh, forgive me, it matters,' Iles said.

Her husband intervened. 'But there's not much now that –'

'It matters considerably,' Iles told them. 'I would like you to understand that this is still very much a live issue with me. My mind is occupied with it all the time.'

'I don't follow,' Street said.

'All the time,' Iles replied.

'Good,' Angela said. 'You're the one I trust, Mr Iles.'

Street tried again: 'Mr Iles, don't you think it would be better now to –'

'Desmond's a great team man,' the Chief said.

'Angela here hopes to come into the police soon, don't you, love?' Mrs Street told them.

Iles took the girl's hand for a second but said nothing and lowered his head. When they found Street's body Harpur had seen the ACC close to weeping and wondered if he would break now.

'Your son worked with Mr Harpur,' Lane said.

'I hear he did well,' Street replied. He was fresh-faced and also heavily made, a Methodist minister, though wearing no dog-collar. How did their son get to be so thin? And Angela was very slim, too, almost slight: a dark-haired, sharp-featured girl of seventeen, happy-looking – even today – and alert. Harpur sensed that like her brother she had a brain and drive.

'Ray was one of our very best undercover people,' he told Street.

'So you'll ask how come he was caught and killed,' Iles muttered.

'No, it's grand to know he succeeded, that's all,' Street replied.

'You're kind to us,' Iles said, 'and we'd dearly like to deserve it. One day we will, we will.'

The Streets moved on with Lane to meet members of the police committee, who had just arrived. Gazing at them, Iles said: 'Look at the suits, Col. There were sharper outfits on the Jarrow March. That turd, Councillor Tobin, scourge of the police, has come, I see. One dead cop equals one pic in the paper.'

Lane was leading the family to front seats.

'Yes, how do we get them now, Colin?' Iles asked.

'Get, sir? Who?'

'Don't play the cretin, Harpur.'

'You mean You-know-who and Favard? Get them?'

'Get them.'

'Harass? How? They keep their cars licensed. He doesn't do it with under-agers in public lavatories. We can't have them for trafficking now. Wood is our only witness and they didn't believe him. The DPP would never wear another case.'

'When I say get I mean get, for God's sake. Deal with ourselves. Or myself. Why should I expect you to be involved? You were only in charge of Street's operation, after all. Considering it carefully, I don't think they ought to be still around when Angela Street joins the police. That would be an insult to her brother and really put the final gloss on our failure. So that has to be my timetable.'

'Sorry, sir. "Still be around": what does that mean?'

Iles ignored this. 'I don't blame you for that court failure, Harpur. You did pretty well everything that was within your capacity. I know I told you to get them at all costs and you didn't. Should I have taken charge personally? Do you really understand how to put the knife in and keep it in? This is an advanced skill, in fact not something learned at all but innate, like the ability to compose the "Emperor" or make a Barry John break. Can I condemn you for being without it? That would be unreasonable and heartless. You've got good protection on Wood, have you? We owe him something, louse or not, after that evidence.'

'An armed man twenty-four hours.'

'I suppose that's enough? It won't be just You-know-who who'll want to get even, you know. He blabbed a lot about a great number of very sensitive and mighty people.'

'The jury didn't believe it, sir, so it's not true.'

'*Touché*. All Woody did was reveal enough about routes to make half the coke carriers in the world afraid their stuff's going to get hijacked by the opposition. They'll love him for that. This warrior of the air is extremely perturbed, as is understandable. Since the acquittals he's been on the phone three times to Celia Mars to tell her how exposed he is, knowing she'll pressure me to coddle him more. She's a very tender-hearted girl and gets upset by such things. She's talking of going to see him and offer comfort. I've banned it, but who knows she'll listen? Col, she could go back to him out of pity, you realize that? I don't have to tell you what women can be like – the mothering bit. This is an ex-lover in very messy trouble. I mustn't lose her. And even if it's only a matter of her making a cheer-up visit there, I'm not happy. That house is dangerous.'

'Are you still doing the crossword with your wife, sir?'

'What? Here we go. The chief's about to tickle the phrasing. Now, give the pretty bog-trotter a chance.'

And, as Iles had forecast, Lane did it very well, including the recitation of some tub-thumping poem ending 'Death thou shalt die', and saying death was not really very much because it couldn't operate without the aid of war or disease or desperate men. So bloody what? It got you just the same. He hoped the poem gave the Streets some comfort, but he wouldn't have bet on it. What Iles was proposing in his raging agony – or what Harpur thought he was proposing – might not comfort Mr and Mrs Street either, though Angela could be a different matter. But it might comfort the ACC more than a poem.

The turn-out was excellent for the unveiling and Harpur felt relieved. Halo parades had never been popular. They reminded people of things they pushed under and would rather keep sunk out of sight. A lot of Ray Street's friends came today, though, and Harpur saw Robert Cotton, Ruth's new husband, among them. Harpur always did what he could to avoid running into him. It hurt that Ruth could belong to someone else.

After the address Lane pulled the unveiling cord and there were drinks. 'You know our old friend and supporter, Maurice Tobin of the police committee, Col?' Iles asked, his arm around the councillor's shoulders. 'It's damn good of you to find time to come and see us in our bad moment today, Maurice, isn't it, Col? Maurice is bothered about morale, a quite understandable anxiety. He wonders whether that jury's blatant anti-police bias has damaged our spirit.'

'That's not at all how I would put it, not at all,' Tobin replied. 'What I am disturbed about is the unwillingness of the jury to accept police evidence.'

'Same thing,' Iles told him. 'But I don't want you or your colleagues to fret about it. We're in good shape. Obviously, we abide by the decision of the court, without question or resentment. Where on earth would law and order be if we did not, I ask. On the other hand, did you get a good look at the people in that jury box? Well, none of them had records, of course, but that only means the buggers are sharp enough to avoid conviction, although as crooked as hell.'

'Please, Mr Iles, several of those people are my constituents.'

'Don't ever turn your back on them, Maurice. We can't afford to lose a chirpy lad like you. But do calm yourself. We bear no grudges. Aren't we used to watching shit-steeped villains walk free? They don't do any of those noble fucking "Rough Justice" BBC programmes about them, do they? We just whistle a merry tune and accept the screaming errors with quiet grace.'

'These are men who have been declared innocent after a long and searching trial,' Tobin replied.

'What are we here for today, then, Maurice?' Iles asked genially. 'One of our boys was killed. Do you think it's a case of delayed cot death? Are you telling me, you a bright-eyed, heavy-duty ponderer with an arts degree from some very well-known place in the north-west – Warrington? – you're telling me that you believe our man and Dandy did each other?'

Lane joined them.

Tobin said: 'I hear Jamieson and Favard have made their first moves towards an action for malicious prosecution by the police. And, of course, they're pushing for an independent public inquiry. It's bad for the Force, bad for the committee, Chief.'

'We'll do what we can to placate them,' Lane replied. 'I've been thinking that as a small gesture it would be nice if Colin went to You-know-who's place personally to return the exhibits, particularly the tasselled silver pencil. This was a heavily disputed section of the evidence and I believe it might help to smooth matters if Colin could take that upon himself.'

Tobin said: 'Ah, yes, the famous pencil. You know, Chief, there were moments when I – ' He paused.

'Yes?' Iles said, brimming with physical threat.

'When I was uneasy,' Tobin finished.

'In what particular respect would that be, Maurice?' Iles inquired.

'How did it really get there, in the outhouse?'

'Not much point in re-running the trial now, is there?' Harpur intervened.

'To be frank, there is a bad smell about this case,' Tobin said. 'The evidence of the informer, Wood, is part of it. So much of that sounded tailored.'

'No, not a smell, a stink,' Iles told him. 'It's the corpse of a dead copper whose murder people want to forget about. And there's another stink, from the filthy breath of the two sods who did it and who can't stop guffawing at the way they got off, and who are probably about to move back into business, taking over Dandy Lorraine's outlets as well.'

'It might be possible to initiate some diplomatic talking with You-know-who and Favard about their grievances at the same time as Colin delivers the exhibits,' Lane said. 'That's the way my mind is running. Let bygones be bygones and so on. It's often a valid part of policing. Things have to be arranged.'

'Good notion, sir,' Iles declared. 'I'll go with Col. A bit of grovelling to crooks always cheers me up, reminds me of my place in the scheme of things. I'll enjoy a chat, and Favard's a sweetie, I hear.'

'I'm not absolutely sure that's a good idea, Desmond,' Lane replied.

'No trouble at all, sir.'

The Chief took Tobin away in case Iles cut loose.

'Thanks plenteously for turning chicken there, Harpur,' Iles snarled. 'Tobin was just going to accuse us of planting when you cut in with your fawning tact. I wanted to hear the droplet actually spell it out before I went for him. Yes, I'll saunter along with you to You-know-who's place, Col. I'd like to get the layout of the house clear in my head. A recce. And lull them a bit, make out we're all buddies now. What was that Lane locution – let bygones be bygones? Pretty. Now I must go to the Streets and make sure none of those intrepid politicians get to them and palsy their day.' He moved off.

Street's parents were being photographed by local papers near the memorial plaque. Angela Street approached Harpur.

'Shouldn't you be in that?' he asked.

'Can't say I really fancy it. Don't know why. Maybe because it looks as if mum and dad have accepted what's happened, settled for a stone obit. It's a pilgrimage to a tomb, OK for crusaders, but Ray wouldn't go much on it, and neither do I. A trip to You-know-who's grave, now, that would be something else.'

'Sometimes it's best to accept a situation, if everything's been tried.'

'Has it?'

'We hit them with everything we had.'

She giggled suddenly. 'Now and then, when I talk to Mr Iles, I think he could kill those two. I mean, literally. Do you get that idea? I mean, you obviously know him so much better than I do. There's something wild in him, but thinking-wild. I like that. It puts fire in his eyes. He cares about Ray, won't let it sleep.'

Harpur sent out for his Dutch uncle voice. 'We're used to keeping the stopper on personal feelings, Angela. You'll learn that when you come in. It's a big part of the job. Police officers are not avengers. They don't hunt people to their deaths.'

'Oh, I suppose it's just the way he talks and looks.' She stared about the room. Iles was right about Tobin, and he and the police committee chairman had joined Mr and Mrs Street for a picture at the Halo Wall. 'I thought Ray's girl would be here,' Angela said. 'Wasn't she invited?'

'It's official family only.'

'Why?'

'That's just the way it – '

'Is she an embarrassment?'

'How so?'

'Oh, I think you know what I mean.'

'No. Because she snorts and may have done a bit of tarting? We wouldn't keep her out for that, honestly. It's just not how these things are arranged, that's all.'

Angela paused for a moment and made an exaggerated, comical swallowing motion. 'OK, can I tell you what I really meant? Friends of Ray who come to see mum and dad say she should have given evidence. She knew something about his last hours.'

'Oh? Your parents haven't mentioned anything like that to me.'

'They wouldn't, would they? They don't like making trouble. They want to get it all into the past and bearable.'

'Where does the information come from?'

'Are you really saying you haven't heard this Mr Harpur? Apparently, she was sounding off about it in some pub brawl after the trial. The Martyr? One of Ray's uniformed friends was called to deal with it, because it turned into a fight, and he got the whole story from her.'

'She's often as high as a kite. She might easily cause a disturbance.'

'Myself, I thought that must be why you couldn't risk her in the box. Ray told me she did a bit.'

'All kinds of reasons we couldn't use her, really, Angela. Mr

Iles didn't regard her as a credible witness.' As he said it he realized how stupid that must sound now when none of them had
been considered credible.

'Some of the people who knew Ray think the case wasn't
really pushed hard against those two because – well, that's
another story.'

'What is?'

She was growing red and had trouble picking her words. 'I'd
rather not. I don't really know enough about it. Rumour and
back-chat. You'd despise all that. I do myself.'

'Christ, but about what?'

'Can we leave it? Please.'

He could have taken hold of her thin shoulders and shaken
her. Harpur wanted to be thought well of by this girl, by any
girl, but especially one with looks. For a moment her voice had
said without saying it that he was shady, tainted. Jesus, did
friends of Street think this case had been soft-pedalled because
someone was on the take, because he was on the take? Did
Street's parents and this girl believe that? Suddenly he started
to sympathize with Iles's determination to get those two, clear
the books, clean the air. Angela could not have heard the same
whisper about Iles or she would not be singing his praises.

Her parents, Tobin and the committee chairman joined
them and Tobin said to Mr and Mrs Street: 'I'm very glad,
very glad indeed, that you can find today a therapy and treat it
as the close of a chapter.'

Behind his back Angela gave a powerful two-fingered up-
you sign.

'We have our occasional disagreements with senior officers,
of course,' Tobin went on, 'but I know we all have the well-
being of the Force at heart, and the well-being of every officer
in it. Is not that so, chief superintendent?'

Harpur turned and spoke to Mr and Mrs Street: 'Try not to
hold it against us.'

Iles came back, beaming and talkative. 'Maurice, you will
look special in those pictures, I know it – a touch of the peas-
ant, in the very best sense: natural dignity, strength and grace.
These should always be the accompaniments of power, cer-

tainly, but I fear it is rarely so.'

Looking at Iles now, Harpur could understand why Angela Street diagnosed that mixture of ferocity and calculation in him. Sometimes Harpur wished he had given more time to sorting out how the Assistant Chief's mind functioned. Could he be pushed into obsession? How much was he capable of – as much as this girl thought? Probably.

'I don't quite understand about police committees,' Angela said. 'What they do, what they are for? I ought to know before I come in.'

Iles became grave. 'Indeed, you must, Angela. Why, they are the true voice of the people, my dear. Maurice and the chairman have been thrown up by the democratic process. Yes, thrown up, isn't that so, Maurice?'

'We control the police on behalf of the electorate,' Tobin told her.

'That's it.' Iles nodded several times, seemingly alight with approval at Tobin's choice of words. 'Maurice controls us. Angela, in that phrase you see another of the natural politician's gifts. It is the ability to put what might appear complex matters into very simple, forthright terms. There's what's known as a chain of command, you see, Angela. It goes up through constables to the senior officers, like Colin, here; then me, then Mr Lane, and then beyond that to Maurice, the chairman and their colleagues. They tell us how to run things. Yes, Maurice and the chairman and so on are actually in charge. They aren't trained, of course, or anything like that, and they have political aims to take account of, but they bring to their work the great, sparkling asset of knowing the people's will, you see.'

Harpur saw the girl was studying Iles's face, obviously amazed that he could pile on the piss-taking but betray there no evidence of his rage and bristling contempt. Somehow in his career Iles must have learned to keep the savagery in him decently screwed down and disguised, or he would not have made it to ACC. If he was able to reduce sex to crossword puzzles he could probably transform his anger into charm. Were the restraints starting to come apart now, though? As

Lane had said, Iles was a great team man, and sometimes it looked to Harpur as if the death of Street had reached his nervous system. It was starting to reach Harpur's, too, now he knew people thought he took payola and connived at Street's death. Lane might also have said that Iles was a committed loather of juries, and these acquittals had possibly taken him a bit closer to eruption.

'So, in a way, Councillor Tobin will be my boss when I join?' Angela asked, helping things along.

'Exactly. Or some other Tobin – should Maurice get kicked out before,' Iles replied. 'They do not go on for ever, not even those with the flair and inborn grandeur of Maurice. It's difficult for us, and for him, of course. What the public think is right one day they think is wrong the next. That's politics. The police have to deal with such matters as right and wrong, you see, and murder and gangsterism. We want to apply abiding standards, if possibe. But it is people like Maurice who let us know what we should really be doing. It's quite a help, stops us from being narrow and consistent. The politician is our flexible friend.'

'We see ourselves as guardians of the public interest in a general sense,' Tobin said.

'Maurice and those like him set a moral tone,' Iles explained. 'That's important for us. We're so busy waving our hands at the traffic and picking up lost dogs, you understand. We need someone weighty, thoughtful, acute, in touch, who is above it all. Frankly, I don't know where we'd be without Maurice.'

14

They had a radio shout from the man looking after Simon Wood in his fine, long house on the cliff and at almost the same time a 999 message from Wood himself. Neither call was completed.

Harpur had not been in the Control Room when it happened, but as they raced towards Wood's place in the Rover, with a driver and another man, Francis Garland told him the sequence. Other cars were far ahead of them.

'Peter Lowry, our guard dog, came on the air just after 4.20 this afternoon to say he was investigating intruders – plural – near Wood's garage, at the far end of the garden. Lowry was speaking from outside. He said he suspected youths or kids fooling, and didn't seem bothered. Well, Christ, this is tea-time, broad daylight. There was no request for aid at that stage. Apparently, he sounded almost apologetic for making the call.' Garland consulted a print out for the rest. 'At 4.24 he called again and now was quite agitated. "Correction. Not children. At least three men. Possible arms. Am compromised. Need aid. They are – " Some unintelligible words followed and it ended there, sir. They tried to get him back, of course, but nothing.'

'Iles said we ought to have more than one man there.'

'And while Lowry was talking on radio, Wood came screaming over the phone, starting at – '

'Can't we put on some speed, Chris?' Harpur snarled. 'Has your mother been telling you to take care again?'

'Wood's call began at 4.22 and he was in a real state – hard to get some of his words, too, but shouting that the house was under attack. He said he had seen people front and back, and then he began yelling that Lowry had deserted him and accused us of deliberately leaving him exposed to earn our backhanders.'

'Jesus.'

The Rover's radio picked up a message from the first car to arrive at Wood's place reporting to Control. 'Alpha Foxtrot Tango: well-established fire in three downstairs rooms and entrance hall. Looking for a way in at back. No sign of occupant.'

Garland took the microphone: 'Hello Alpha Foxtrot Tango, this is Master. Look for two occupants, repeat two, one male, one female.'

'Roger.'

Garland said to Harpur: 'At the end of his phone call Wood

was saying he had someone with him in the house, visiting – a
woman. What he called "a special woman the police wouldn't
want to see hurt". Control told him they were coming with
everything they had, of course, and that there was a car not too
far from him. He yelled it was too late and that people were
inside the place already. Then he said, "They're tearing the – "
and nothing more. Control assumed he wanted to say they
were ripping out the phone wires. The number was unobtain-
able when they rang back. Isn't Desmond Iles doing something with a girl who used to belong to Wood?'

'Celia Mars. He's going to be very, very sick if she's hurt.'

'I'm glad I'm not still seeing Sarah Iles then. I wouldn't want
venereal contact with Wood, however distant. So, could Celia
be at Wood's house?'

'It's possible. Yes, it's likely. Does Iles know about the
calls?'

'He's refereeing a police rugby cup game in Wales.'

The Rover ripped a bumper from a parked car and it rattled
and clanged with them for a few hundred yards. 'Sounds like a
Skoda,' Harpur said. The Rover did not slacken pace for a
second.

Garland said: 'Christ, a fire attack in broad daylight.'

'No names from either of them?'

'Nothing.'

'Would Lowry recognize You-know-who or Favard?'

'Everyone guarding Wood has been shown pictures.'

'I need someone at You-know-who's place at once,' Harpur
decided. 'We'll want to watch the buggers come back. They
could be scorched and stinking of fire-lighters and cordite and
who knows what?'

'Yes, I've sent a couple of lads, sir.'

The Rover stopped in front of Wood's house. Smoke
stretched and billowed in a wind off the sea, and timber
crackled like a firing range. By now the flames seemed to have
taken hold of most of the ground floor, but three firemen in
breathing apparatus were preparing to go in at a side door.

The two men from Alpha Delta Foxtrot came wearily
towards Harpur from the house, their eyes red and both with

131

smoke-grimed faces and scorch holes in their uniforms. The sergeant said: 'We could only look in the back room, sir – the kitchen and a little sitting room – and there was nobody there. Too fierce to get to the front or the stairs. The place reeks of petrol. It looked as if furniture had been piled in the hall. They knew what they were doing. Boys from one of the other cars have gone down to the garage looking for Lowry.'

The roaring of the flames increased suddenly and, as they watched, part of the upper floor tilted steeply and crashed through, and at once the middle of the house was a solid block of red from roof to ground. The three firemen who had gone in emerged suddenly at the side door, all looking very shaky and two supporting each other. Harpur and Garland went closer and tried to see into the long front room past firemen with three hoses pouring water through the windows. Had there been a telephone in that room? Harpur tried to remember. Wood might have been attacked while trying to make his call.

They were helping the injured fireman remove his mask and then they walked him slowly to an ambulance.

The fire-fighting chief spoke hurriedly to Harpur. 'My men saw a woman's body in there but the upstairs floor came down before they could reach it. She made no movement, and they think she was already dead. I've had to abandon searching for the time being.'

'Nobody could be alive in there,' Garland said.

'We don't say things like that until we've looked,' the fireman replied.

Another section of the upper floor gave way, hung for half a minute while torching pieces of furniture slid and fell, then itself plunged down, and the smoke thickened until a great triangle of sparks arose, thrusting its point high above what was left of the roof.

'We understand that at least six people might be inside,' the fire chief said. 'Is that your information?'

Momentarily Harpur was puzzled. 'I thought two.'

'The owner, a woman friend, a police officer and at least three intruders.'

'We think the officer was outside, near the garage. I'd assumed the intruders started the fire and left.'

'I never assume anything.' The fire chief went to one of the hose teams.

'Ever seen a prick in a white helmet before, Francis?' Harpur asked, loud enough, but the fire chief did not turn.

Men began shouting from near the garage, crouched over something in the ferns. Harpur and Garland hurried to them. It was Peter Lowry, lying on his back, eyes staring, his shirt red and sopping from what looked like five, perhaps six, knife wounds in his chest. Nearby, his radio lay half buried in the soft soil, as if someone had ground at it with his heel. Harpur bent down and gingerly opened Lowry's jacket. The shoulder holster underneath was empty, but his .38 was not in Lowry's hand, nor anywhere nearby.

'There goes the rest of the roof,' Garland said. It fell with a heavy, muted thud, like a far-off explosion, and now the smoke triangle became a great arc which hung over the house for a few minutes, almost perfectly symmetrical, then subsided.

'What's that bum in the white hat supposed to be doing?' Harpur asked. 'It's worse since he started.'

On the way back to headquarters they called at Celia Mars's flat, but could get no answer, and then went on to You-know-who's place. The men sent by Garland were watching there and reported that the house seemed empty.

'We can't put out a warrant, can we?' Garland asked as they drove away. 'Nothing concrete to connect them. And we're not going to have much forensic left after the fire.'

'What's it all about, sir?' Chris, the driver, asked.

'They wanted Wood for old times' sake,' Harpur said. 'Anyone in the way or with him got it, too.'

'They wanted him as badly as that?' At the house, Chris had followed them down to look at Lowry's body.

'Wood tried to put them away,' Harpur replied.

'Yes, I know, but – '

'They would have been souped up,' Garland said.

'He did them big damage,' Harpur added. It was true what Iles had said: even though the jury had not believed in Wood,

133

there were plenty of people around the world who would be very glad of the information he gave, drug-runners and foreign police.

For a while, Chris drove in silence. 'I suppose the buggers feel pretty safe, sir. We missed them once, and now they think they're fireproof. Not like Simon Wood.'

'We'll nail them this time.'

Chris stayed silent.

'I tell you we will.'

Again nobody replied and, in the pause, Harpur tried to work out how Iles would react when he knew Celia Mars had been killed and he was back to murmuring sweet adobes to Sarah, if she still wanted them and him. The range of what Iles might do was so huge and terrible that Harpur gave up.

Once more the radio suddenly came alive and they all tensed as a patrol car out near Romer called headquarters.

'Delta Zulu to control: am in pursuit of grey BMW, model 635csl, registration A78 WWW, containing four males probably white. Vehicle broke through Romer road-block. Pursued vehicle has offside rear wing damaged. Am proceeding north from Romer towards Theakin on B7718.'

'Roger, Delta Zulu. Will send aid. Come in Alpha Victor.'

'Alpha Victor: I hear you.'

'Hello Alpha Victor. Intercept grey BMW, registration A78 WWW, travelling north towards you on B7718 and approaching Theakin. Delta Zulu in pursuit. Damaged offside rear wing. Detain four male occupants. Exercise caution. Possible firearms.'

'Shall we join them, Chris?' Harpur said, and the driver turned into a side-street, circled the block and sped north, siren singing. 'They ought to have been through and away an hour ago.'

'They must have been lying low somewhere,' Garland suggested. 'Or they've had car trouble.'

'If it's them,' Harpur said. 'Joyriders like going through road-blocks. Are you carrying anything?'

'No, sir.'

'Nor me, sod it.'

Garland found a map. 'They're in rough country. Plenty of forest, with tracks able to take rally cars.'

'Jesus, this could turn out a crew of speed-mad yobs.'

'If it is, sir, they'll have the fun scared out of them for ever.'

A helicopter was following the road ahead.

Delta Zulu spoke. 'Turning west from B7718 on to B1424, three miles south of Theakin and now proceeding towards Pendar.'

After a minute, Control responded. 'All units in Pendar area prepare road-block at junction of B1424 and B6161 at Gillhope. Close road completely. Repeat, close road completely.'

'Might have a bit of bent metal here,' the man in the front with Chris muttered.

Squinting at the map with a pencil torch, Garland said: 'Chris, if we take Maiden Lane we get straight through to Gillhoe, don't we, avoiding Black Hill?'

'It's OK if there are no farm vehicles.'

'Getting late for that. Let's risk it.'

Giving orders was Garland's strong suit, but they usually made sense. 'Yes, try it, Chris,' Harpur said.

After a couple of miles, they took the turning into a high-hedged, single-track winding road and Chris started working very hard with the wheel and brakes.

Delta Zulu said: 'Losing him.'

Garland looked back at the map. 'That's all right. He can't turn now. He's got to go towards the block.'

'Or take this road from the far end,' Harpur suggested.

'Jesus, would he?' Chris said.

'If he knows the country he might,' Harpur answered, 'and You-know-who ought to know it, he's a local.'

Chris kept the speed up all the same. The man in the front passenger seat crouched forward, as if trying for an early view around the bends, or maybe listening for the roar of a high-quality approaching engine.

'Is You-know-who mad?' Garland asked. 'To dodge a life sentence and then risk all this?'

'They've got two rules, people like You-know-who,' Harpur replied. 'Get your share, and settle with finks, and settling is even more important than getting your share. If they don't do it, and make sure everyone sees they do it, the whole system could come to pieces because of betrayals.'

'Vengeance is mine saith the hood.'

'All sorts like vengeance,' Harpur replied. 'It can take a hold.'

Garland glanced at him.

'Yes, even on me,' Harpur said. 'They've made us look dirty. How else do we put it right?'

They were through Maiden Lane without trouble.

'Wait at the end, so they can't turn into it,' Garland told Chris. 'When they pass, we get behind and drive them into the block. We're bound to be ahead of them.'

Delta Zulu was obviously concentrating on speed and had given no location report for minutes. It had begun to get dark. In Maiden Lane, Chris had driven with headlights on to signal their coming. Now, he switched off altogether but kept the engine running. Harpur felt as he had all those months ago when they sat in the Granada waiting for a gang raid at Lloyd's Bank. Chris had been the driver then, too, and Garland one of the crew. There were differences. When Harpur waited that day he could take a mite of comfort from the presence of a .38 nestling against his chest, even if he did hate guns. They lowered the windows now so they would hear the BMW sooner.

'There'll be a tyre lever in the boot,' Garland said. Chris switched off and gave him the keys. When Garland came back he offered the metal bar to Harpur, who took it. If anybody was to be done one day for using non-regulation weapons it had better be the man in charge. In any case, he would enjoy taking the steel to You-know-who's structure. Harpur had a lot to say with it, from Ray Street, from Mr and Mrs Street and Angela, and something from Iles, too, though if Iles were back from imposing fair play and reasonableness in the rugby game he would want to say and do it all himself, and even more so when he heard about Celia.

'Here she comes,' Garland said.

They all picked up the sound of the BMW, making fine

pace, but no other vehicle. Delta Zulu must really have been left.

'That's a pro driver,' Chris decided.

'They've hired experts,' Harpur said. 'You-know-who always does. Look at Larnog QC.' He saw the car now, making pretty much a ton, regardless of the road, no lights, holding the middle and never deviating from its line. Would there be a decent, straight run-in to the road-block so the BMW could sight it early? If not, and they hit it at that speed there would be no unwelding flesh from steel afterwards. Perhaps this was the easiest way to write an end. He would regret that, though. He certainly wanted You-know-who and Favard hurt, and catastrophically hurt, but hurt if possible by the law and in the law's proper fashion, helped if need be by some spruced-up evidence, yet with all the seemly processes doing their public bit. If that turned out impossible eventually, something other might be necessary, and Iles would probably emerge as the something other. Fair enough. A road accident would not be the same kind of tidy reprisal. Forcing someone into a crusher, even someone like You-know-who, lacked definition, did not say clearly and firmly enough that in the long run, and sometimes even in the short run, the coppers won and had a good future. Ideally, there had to be the braying, slippery fuckers in wigs if that message was really going to get across to Madam Vox Pop. Failing that, a vengeance tableau might have to be privately arranged. What was crucial then was that everyone, and especially everyone in the police, should recognize it as a piece of vengeance. Getting someone to bang into a road-block would be crude and vague and unsatisfying.

The BMW was almost on them and suddenly its speed fell sharply and the car seemed to start a swerve. For a second, Harpur thought the driver had lost control and maybe hit something in the road and been shoved off course.

'Christ, you're right, sir, he is making for here,' Barry said, from alongside the driver. 'They haven't seen us.'

'No way they'll get round,' Chris yelled.

'Use your lights,' Harpur yelled, and Chris hit the swtich.

The beams caught the BMW like a searchlight finding an

aircraft and Harpur saw at once that the men in the front were not You-know-who and Favard. The two behind he could not make out.

For another second the BMW surged towards them, as if the driver had been transfixed by the sudden glare, and then he half-braked and tugged the wheel over, trying to turn away and get back to his course. There were the beginnings of a skid and the rear of the car started to swing around. Harpur thought the vehicle would hit them broadside on and he prepared himself for the impact. But once their driver had the nose of the car moving away from the Rover he released the brake and put his foot hard on the juice again. They sidled a couple more yards but the power of the engine had hold again now and the BMW pulled away, its speed climbing fast.

'Yes, a pro,' Chris said.

'Let's get behind,' Harpur said. They heard Delta Zulu not far off and saw its lights come and go as it took the bends. Chris pulled out.

For a few miles they kept close enough to have the BMW in sight, but soon it started to leave them, getting in and out of the turns faster than Chris could manage with the Rover. The BMW was still unlit, so once they lost it they had no gleams through the hedges and trees.

After six minutes they drew up at the Gillhope road-block, with Delta Zulu right after them. Uniformed men with pistols and shot-guns appeared warily from behind the barricade of cars and farm trucks. The block looked entirely intact and the men were still obviously keyed up, waiting for the BMW to show.

Garland had the map out again. 'Nowhere they could have turned off – not a cart-track even.'

'Did you get a sound of it?' Harpur asked the inspector running the block.

'You were the first vehicle we heard or saw, sir.'

So they had left the road at least three or four miles back.

'They could have driven into a field, waiting for the two of us to pass and gone back the other way,' Garland suggested.

The chopper idled overhead. On the other side of the block

Alpha Victor arrived at speed. This operation was beginning to look like farce, nicely illuminated by the helicopter's spotlight.

Chris turned the Rover and they prepared to move. On the way back they would take things more slowly. Harpur told Control the BMW had disappeared and might be pointing towards the battalion of support that would be on its way to Gillhope. At Control there would be a lot of very heavy cursing. How the hell did two units lose a car on an end-stopped, no-exits B road? All that came back from Control, though, was: 'Roger, are you continuing search?'

'Continuing,' Harpur replied. 'Request helicopter look at fields and woods bordering B1424,' and in a moment the chopper swung away, its beam still probing down, and began patterned flights across both sides of the road.

At every farm gate now, the Rover pulled in and they looked for tyre marks in the mud and stared out across the fields for as far as they could see. It was not very far. Full darkness had come and thick, grey cloud hung low and gave occasional bursts of fine, dense rain, bringing visibility down even more. The ground was still reasonably firm and it might have been possible for a car to make a decent distance. If they had crossed a field, though, there would be clear tracks.

And that was how they ultimately located the BMW. Suddenly the search had changed its nature. No longer a car chase, it had turned into that oldest kind of pursuit, the hunt for men on foot, men probably deep in cover by now, using a vast patch of mountainside forest which loomed ten minutes' trot away from the abandoned vehicle. So that things would look normal from the road, they had taken the trouble to shut the gate behind them. Around the gate, their tyre marks merged with others, but then went their way towards the edge of the field and the forest. Chris drove in the tracks and after about a quarter of a mile they saw the BMW stopped ahead, obviously empty, its front passenger door wide open.

Garland spoke to the chopper and in a couple of minutes it was above them and moving off to see what it could through the trees. It would be little. These boys from the BMW knew what they were doing.

'We'll have a cordon right around and we'll need dogs, Francis,' Harpur said. 'Tell Control I want the forest surrounded but not entered. A few of us will go in and drive the buggers out. Otherwise we'll have our people popping off at one another.'

Garland relayed the instructions.

'Roger,' Control answered. 'Mr Iles is now in the building and will join you soonest. Please give your exact location.'

'Jesus,' Garland muttered, but not on the air.

Harpur said: 'As a matter of fact, he manages a very *svelte* rural sweep.'

'Do I tell him where we are?'

'What else?'

When Iles arrived, it was in a stream of police traffic as men for the cordon, dogs and sharpshooters assembled at the edge of the forest. For a few minutes the ACC remained in his Cavalier, head lowered, not looking at the scene outside. This was unlike him. A savage, brilliant energy normally held Iles, forcing him always towards action. Harpur watched him, but did not approach or interrupt.

Then Iles sat up properly, gazed about and left the car. 'I went over to Wood's place,' he told Harpur.

'I thought you might, sir.'

'They've pulled out the bodies now. Some jerk who talks like a breviary in charge.'

'I met him.'

Iles turned away for a moment and spoke at first without looking at Harpur. 'I'd told Celia twenty times not to go to the house. She thought it just jealousy and small-mindedness, which, all right, partly it was. But only part.' He turned back towards Harpur. 'I suggested that if she really needed to see Wood because she was worried about him he could go to her place or they could meet in a pub. Anywhere but that bloody target house. She had to do things her way, though. She made up her own mind. It was a quality I loved in her, even if it did mean making up her mind to nurse that septic mouth, Wood.'

The helicopter roared right above, hovering for a time. Iles talked on, apparently not able to stop, but Harpur heard none of it. When the chopper dipped off towards the trees again, Iles was saying, 'had intended leaving Sarah pretty soon to set up properly with Celia. Of course, that would probably have meant jacking in the job, too, which would have upset me, rather. All for love, though. There seemed no other way.'

'It must have been –'

'Deep? Yes, deep, Col. It all developed damn fast. And was ended by these sods damn fast. You know how such things can happen, for God's sake. You still seeing Ruth?'

'She re-married, sir.'

'Don't I know that? I was at the wedding, wasn't I, and pulled the two of you out of your hidey-hole in the nick of time and directed you back to respectability? I asked if you were still seeing her. Of course you are. These things are not stopped by a bit of church rigmarole and a three-wine reception, are they? They're powerful. They come out of nowhere – start in game-playing, and suddenly you're lost. Or I was. You – you're a cold one, maybe, and able to keep it all limited. Yes, a cold item, I'd say, but none the worse for that, Col.'

One of the Alsatians began barking at him and showing its teeth, tugging at its leash, as if determined to attack, and Iles bent down to the animal, murmuring solace and comfort. 'I wouldn't touch her, sir,' the handler said.

Iles put his hand on the Alsatian's neck and stroked it gently, still murmuring. The dog quietened and turned its head and licked him.

'Col, what I want to find out, and what I'm going to find out, is which of these four pulled the trigger on Celia. They can't make much out from the body – ' His voice went for a couple of seconds and he suddenly gripped Harpur's shoulder for support. 'Sorry, Col.' He released the hold almost at once. 'They believe Celia was shot twice in the back. Wood, too, as if anyone could give a toss. Might be the same gunman, or they could have taken it in turns. We've got an account for Ray Street, Peter Lowry and Celia to tidy up, Col, and that must take in all these four, I should think. But the one who did Celia – that's very important to me, and I suppose I'd like one of them left alive at the end so he can tell me who it was.'

'We want them all alive, sir, obviously.'

'Ah, it's piety time, is it? Do you mean, Harpur, you'd risk putting them in front of a jury again, give another handful of bent glory and fees to Larnog QC? No, I think the general rule has to be this time, make it stick by blowing their bloody heads off, but try to knock one of them over in such a way that while he's bleeding to death he can tell me which one did it to my lovely girl, so I'll know it's OK. Now, you're going to argue that if we take the scalps off all four it will be OK, too, because we'll be sure to have included the one who got Celia. That's reasonable, I don't deny it, but it wouldn't be quite perfect, Col, because in that case I'd be unable to look at his body, the specific body, with the specific holes in it and assess the specific pain the wounds give him, I hope. About that there'd be a kind of exactness, and we need it.'

'Yes, I understand.'

'You say that.'

'I feel it, sir.'

'Well, grand. We'll make a cop of you yet, Colin. Those bleeding firemen were speculating that Celia must be what they called Wood's "live-in woman". Their information said he wasn't married, so they wanted some explanation for her being there. All right, she did live with him once – God knows how it came about – but would those scruffy, scorched bastards understand she was simply present now to help another human being out of a black patch? Does there have to be sex in everything? Schweitzer in the white helmet said he thought people should not make guesses about the woman, but you could see he thought the same. I hit nobody, Col, and called none of them the malign shits they are. I ask you, how could I cut up nasty when her body was there like a slab of charred turf? Celia was only a kid, you know, not thirty. I adored her. She saw something in me, though God knows what or why. Where's the map, Col? I've got a few suggestions about cornering them, though it's your show absolutely, that goes without saying.'

'I suppose we'd better keep in mind, sir, that we have as yet no – '

Iles held up a hand to stop Harpur. 'You're going to say there's no established link between the men from the BMW and the killing of my girl and Street and Lowry and what's his name. A reasonable point, Col, as ever, and reasonably made. But that's a load of pedantic cock, isn't it, Harpur? You and I know these are the right men. We know, as certainly as we know Johnny Mercer to be a genius, that You-know-who and Favard and a couple of home helps did these jobs, don't we? Of course we bloody do. So, where's the map?'

'Francis had it.'

'Garland? I suppose he had to be here. Things weren't raw enough without that?'

Men and dogs had begun stringing out around the edge of the forest. Far away, on the opposite side, other men and dogs would be doing the same.

Garland gave Iles the map. 'Many thanks, Francis. Wonderful to see you. At least you can't be humouring someone's wife while you're up here in gumboots.' He spread the map on top of the Rover. 'A bit of a reservoir here, look, Col. If we could ease them down that way they might finish up in the water, which would be a simplification. Do you think fluoride would stand much of a chance against the poison in You-know-who? Or they might have to run for it along this path at the edge, which has very little cover and is elevated. They'd be like cans on a wall. Naturally, we must get them to fire first. There are basic decencies which I don't lose sight of. And then in retaliation it's open-house, yes? I thought we could go in together, Col. I've always loved walking in woods, regardless of Hansel and Gretel. There's a Smith and Wesson Airweight for you in the car.'

When Harpur had checked the cordon was right round, he and Iles led the hunt party in. They took Garland, three marksmen and three dogs with their handlers. Iles carried a loud hailer and had moved his pistol from the shoulder-holster to the pocket of his waterproof in case he needed it in a rush. This was the kind of operation that should have waited until daylight, but Harpur knew Iles would not wear that, and he was not sure he could have put up with the delay himself.

As a precaution against shooting they kept big spaces between them and used the flashlights sparingly, except for Iles who had his own tactics to follow. They made no effort to curtail noise. That was their chief weapon: they were beaters, meant to drive the quarry ahead by the din, or to terrorize them into giving away their position by opening fire in panic.

Garland came alongside Harpur. 'This is hopeless. So black. We'll lose one another.'

'Want to tell Iles?'

'Who's the boss, sir?'

'Me.'

'Well?'

'He'd go by himself if the rest of us waited. I'm not having that grieving showman cornering the credit.'

Periodically Iles called on the loud hailer. Each time he did he put his flashlight on the ground pointing at himself, offering a target they could pick up by sound and sight. He wanted them to try it. 'This is the police,' he called. 'I am Assistant Chief Constable Desmond Iles. We know it's you out there Cliff Jamieson and Paul Favard. Come now, we're old friends. We understand each other, don't we? This is no place for grown-up people, a bloody wood in the middle of the night. You're surrounded and your position is hopeless. You can't escape. You should surrender at once.' He offered no instructions how to do it, though, because that was not what he aimed for. The loud hailer was only another part of the beating gear, meant to jab the nerves and make them crack. He wouldn't want men coming forward with their hands up and entitled to decent treatment. That was what the courts gave, and he had seen enough of it.

For about three hours they walked, rested, walked again, and then the three Alsatians suddenly grew very excited, tugging hard all in the same direction, snarling and baying.

'Looks juicy,' Iles said. 'We should be close to the reservoir. Over the top of this slope, I'd imagine.' He went through his routine with the flashlight and loud hailer again, standing longer than ever in view, staring out into the dark looking for movement. The dogs hurried up the incline, a couple of the sharpshooters with automatic rifles immediately behind them.

They came to the top. Iles was right and the reservoir stretched beneath them, grey, long, narrow and very still, now and then catching the light from the moon when it escaped the clouds. The dogs had become almost uncontrollable.

'There they go,' Garland said. He had night-glasses with him. 'Down almost at the water's edge.' He pointed. Harpur just made out four figures running and stumbling, line-ahead, apparently unaware they had been spotted.

Iles took the glasses. 'They look all-in.' He paused, still holding the glasses on them. 'I'm trying to sort out which is You-know-who.' He watched for another minute and then abruptly turned to the dog-handlers. 'Let them go.' And while Harpur was thinking about countermanding it the three animals began bounding towards the reservoir. Iles led the gallop after them, hurtling down the incline, fit and sure on his feet, as if he had trained at fell-running every day for this.

Harpur called the cordon to come in around the reservoir, then tried to catch up with Iles and the rest. The Airweight bumped against his thigh in a waist-holster, its flap buttoned down, and he hoped he could keep it like that. Now, he felt a terrible excitement, those frenetic high-spirits of the hue and cry, more potent than anything he ever experienced in a car chase, and more worrying: he recognized it as an odious thrill linked to bullying, gang comradeship and violence, and going right back to school, where a crowd would pursue one odd kid or a few and knock hell out of them when they were caught. Where the hell did that worthy, guilt-ridden thought come from? These were men who had killed, not some misfit child in the playground. They might kill again, too.

The dogs had been silent as they raced down the slope, but now it sounded as if they had caught up with the four. From not far away there was a burst of barking, snarling, shouting, and then a series of rapid shots from hand-guns. Harpur ran faster, suddenly scared that he could see why Iles had ordered the dogs loose. These four might shoot to defend themselves against the Alsatians, and Iles could then call for retaliation.

Harpur had lost sight of the ACC. He would be down somewhere on the right and ahead, perhaps out alone in front, or with a marksman. The helicopter rattled across in front of him, poking about with its light close to the water, but it looked as if the men had somehow found a bit of cover, and the chopper circled and criss-crossed feverishly, getting nowhere. Iles had expected them to use the embankment around the water's edge, silhouetting themselves for target practice, but they had more sense.

Harpur fell badly. He was running through scrub and fern, keeping his eyes on where he thought the men must be and not watching the ground. His shoulder hit a half-buried rock and pain roared through his body so that for a second he felt he might black out. He forced himself to stand at once and retched twice. Christ, the din would alert the county. Then, very near him, the ferns stirred violently, and he turned quickly to face whatever it was, grabbing awkwardly around his body for the holster with his left hand because his right hung numb at his side after the fall. Tugging the flap open, he put his hand on the butt of the Airweight and crouched. The movement in the ferns was not repeated, though, and after a minute he moved carefully towards the spot, still keeping down.

He found one of the Alsatians, bleeding from three wounds in the side, and dead now. It had been the animal's death kicks that frightened him. Nearby, he found the body of another of the dogs and decided this was what had tripped him. He remained motionless, getting a grip on the nausea and listening, in case the third Alsatian was alive somewhere and still harassing the four. Perhaps he did hear barking, from a long way off, and then sporadic shouting, too distant to identify voices. The helicopter swept over at just above tree height and temporarily all other sound was lost. While waiting for his arm and hand to get some feeling back, he remained crouched for a couple of seconds longer. Then he moved off towards where the shouting had come from, taking care now, not galloping.

Almost immediately then he saw ahead three or four men lying in the shrub. They were facing away from Harpur and seemed to be staring at something below. Very quietly, Harpur

edged forward. God, his open-country stalking would be fron-
tiersman standard after this. Once again he put his hand on the
Airweight, though by now he had the use of his right. He did
not draw the gun.

In a moment, he thought he recognized Garland, from the
shape of his head and his jacket. Then he saw that two of the
other men had rifles and realized they must be marksmen.
Nearby on the ground he made out the loud hailer that Iles had
been using. Harpur whistled gently and Garland turned, then
beckoned him forward and Harpur crawled to a position between him and the marksmen. Now, he could see what
interested them below. It was a single-storey, stone-clad windowless building belonging to the reservoir people and hous-
ing equipment.

'They've broken in,' Garland said. 'We've got them.'

'Where's Iles?'

Garland pointed and Harpur saw the ACC moving skilfully
down the last part of the slope towards the building. Another
of the marksmen accompanied him. Iles had a pistol in his
hand.

'He's going to what he calls "parley with them", sir,' Garland told him. 'These boys are to give cover.' Garland himself
was not armed. 'Those four are probably in a panic. We think
most of their ammo's gone on the dogs.'

'If not, this could be the bloody OK Corral.'

'It's how Iles wanted it, sir. I couldn't stop him, could I?'

'Have we got identifications yet?'

'No, sir. Presumably You-know-who, Favard and two
anons.'

'Christ, Francis, it's a mess.'

'How so, sir? We know they're not the Babes in the Wood.
They've broken road-blocks and they use hand-guns.' He
pointed to a spot near the building and Harpur saw the third
Alsatian's body. 'There's not really any question, is there, that
they did Lowry, Wood and Celia Mars?'

'Not much question, but some question. And killing dogs is
no topping offence. I'm not having Iles provoking a shoot-out
here.' At once, Harpur stood up in full view, walked to the

147

loud hailer and pointed it towards the building. 'You four men in the water-authority property,' he called. 'You are surrounded by armed police. The helicopter has your location. You cannot escape. A cordon is closing in. Come out now without your weapons, and with your hands on your head. I repeat: leave your weapons inside and come out with your hands on your head. I give you my word that you will be in no danger. This is Chief Superintendent Harpur, in charge of the operation. Come out now and stand still in front of the building.' He saw Iles stop and stare back at him, rage filling his face. Harpur put down the loud hailer and waited. It had begun to grow light. After a few seconds there was some small movement at the back of the building. A man appeared, hands on his head, shuffling very slowly, as if scared any quicker movement might be mistaken as an attempt at escape. He stood alone in front of the building, looking up the slope at Harpur.

For a couple of minutes nobody joined him and Harpur had bent down to pick up the hailer again when two more men came out just as slowly, hands on their heads. Then, almost as soon as the three were in line, Harpur heard a single shot and groaned in horror, thinking at first that Iles must have fired. But after a minute he realized that the noise had come from inside the little store building. All three of the men waiting outside spun around, but none re-entered.

Garland was standing alongside Harpur now and had the glasses up. 'None of these three is You-know-who or Favard. Nobody I recognize.'

Iles had resumed his descent, the pistol still in his hand, and the marksman at his heels. Harpur started to move down towards the building, too.

Garland went with him. 'You handled that right, sir – if I may say.'

'Well, I'm feeling pretty smug.'

By the time they reached the building Iles had the three men lying on the ground and was personally searching them while a marksman stood guard, the rifle cradled across his chest. Iles pulled a six-shot Astra from the pocket of one of the men and, kneeling beside him, spun the chamber around. It was empty. The ACC went on to his hands and knees, put his mouth against the ear of the captured man and whispered something. It looked like a picture Harpur had seen in childhood of a stretcher-bearer during the First World War crouched over a casualty in no man's land.

But the man kept his head turned away from Iles and did not attempt to speak. The ACC pushed his face forward and this time bellowed at full power in the man's ear: 'I'm talking to you, gallows bird. Are you receiving me, sweet lad? All I want to know is, who killed the girl? Not Wood or even the cop. I don't ask you that. Just tell me who killed the girl. This is the gun that did it?' He struck the man hard behind the ear with the barrel. 'All bullets spent. Four for the dogs and before that two for the girl? You know, you really look to me like the kind of warrior who would blast a pretty woman for no reason.'

Harpur and Garland stepped over another one of the men and went to the door at the back of the building. Lights burned inside. On the floor, under a bank of control dials, the fourth man lay with another Astra stuck in what used to be his mouth. It would be hard to guess what he had looked like, but this was certainly not You-know-who or Favard. He was about twenty-seven. The clothes, shoes and haircut looked expensive London, whereas the particles of him stuck to the walls and dials told nothing about geography or life-style but spoke a general message only, to do with the sudden, unresolvable troubles mankind could run into. Harpur went through the pockets of the pretty, single-breasted suit and found nothing, as he had expected.

Iles came in and looked at the body. 'A sweet disorder in the face. Of course, all that trio out there say this boy did Celia, not to mention Lowry and Wood. We can work on them, however – ardently. North London maggots, bought by the hundredweight. Thanks more than duly for fucking up the whole thing with that broadcast, Harpur. We're right back to Nowheresville because of you.'

'We could have had four dead and no chance of finding anything, sir,' Garland said.

'Ah, Francis. Lovely to hear the voice of reason at dawn on the water's marge,' Iles replied. 'Who said he knew about nothing but adultery? Was it you, Harpur? There's a tactician here.'

'Will those three say Jamieson was their paymaster, sir?' Harpur asked.

'Not yet they won't, but they will.'

Iles sat down on the floor, not far from a pool of blood and bone fragments, and gazed at the body. 'Perhaps they're right, those three, and it was this one. Why else would he do that to himself? If you destroy a lovely kid for no reason, it's bound to get to your soul, isn't it, even the sort of soul issued to this? I mean, someone looks at a face like Celia's and then puts two bullets in her – what kind of peace is he ever going to get after that? Only this kind,' he said, pointing his thumb at the carcass.

'Come on, sir, you'll get piles from sitting on stone,' Garland said, helping him up.

'Thanks, Francis. Not that I see this as the end. Well, obviously not. Someone gave the orders and we know it was You-know-who and You-know-who will know we know. I'll be working on that, and there'll be no bloody call from a loud hailer next time, warning I'm on the way.'

A message from the unit at You-know-who's place said he and Favard had now returned.

'Let us go and make our visit,' Iles suggested.

They changed from their search gear and Harpur went with Iles and Garland in the ACC's car, leaving the Rover to help transport the prisoners. At Nightingale House, Favard opened the door.

'It's three buggers from the framing factory,' he called back over his shoulder.

You-know-who appeared from a back room in cord jacket and slacks, looking mild and apologetic. 'Well, ask them in, Paul. And how about not talking like that?'

'We're here to return a silver, tasselled pencil of yours, Cliff,' Iles told him. 'I've been carrying it about for some time. We wanted a properly representative, and at the same time high-ranking, group to bring it. I expect you recall the item. It was found near a couple of dead bodies.'

'Or maybe not,' Favard said.

Iles brought out a slim, red leather-covered box and presented it. 'We tried to get hold of you throughout yesterday, Cliff. There was an accident to a friend of yours, Simon Wood. Well, a second accident, I suppose we must call it.'

'Ah, I heard. I'm sorry. I'm not next of kin, though, you know. We were away yesterday, as a matter of fact.'

'At Favard's aunty's?' Harpur asked.

'Not at all,' You-know-who replied, laughing. 'But there's no urgency over this, I take it? How about let's go into the drawing-room? I love having guests so I can use it.'

They sat down in bulky leather furniture and Iles gazed up at the ceiling. 'Would this be directly under the room where you did Ray Street, Cliff? I expect you remember that quaint scene in *Tess* when the blood comes through from above after she's knocked off Angel?'

You-know-who poured malt whiskys. 'As a matter of fact, we was up at Kate's, that's my wife, ex-wife, really. My boy Pete's sixth birthday. A big party, of course. I likes to keep in touch. The whole works – magician, caterers, even the vicar turned up.'

'So great a cloud of witnesses,' Iles said.

'Then Kate threw a dinner for the adults in the evening,' Jamieson continued.

'And you stayed for that?' Harpur asked.

'Oh, naturally. I'm only an ex-husband, sure, but I'm still friends with a lot of Kate's acquaintances.'

'Nice,' Iles remarked. 'So you're beautifully alibied for all day and most of the night. I imagine there might be a couple of video tapes of proceedings, with calendars and clocks in the background, just as clinchers?'

'Ah, you're still thinking about that character, Wood, and the cop and the girl,' You-know-who replied. 'When we heard it on the car radio I said to Paul you might put two and two together and come up with another wrong answer. Naturally, we been expecting a call.'

'Of course, we got the four you paid to do it,' Iles remarked. 'Hear that, too?'

'Come on now, Mr Iles. Woody really crossed a lot of very big people with all that rubbish you got him to spout in the box, people here and abroad. That was folks' livings, and high livings. They can turn very unforgiving, people like that. Woody must of known what risks he was into. It could be all sorts behind them killings and the fire.'

'We'll be putting a gentle query or two to these lads we picked up right afterwards,' Iles replied. 'Perhaps your name will get a mention from them.'

'I heard one grew suicidal.'

Harpur said: 'We'd like to – '

'Would I get myself into anything of that sort after all I went through no time ago on account of you boys?' Jamieson asked. 'I'd want my head read, wouldn't I?'

'Cliff, you might have come to feel that you can't go wrong,' Iles replied. 'That's the danger. You've got this lovely house, wife and kids – but a comfortable distance away – a devoted sidekick like Favard who sticks with you whatever you do to him, no doubt a supply of chubby boys on tap, and in your big court triumph a bent and pissed jury who saw everything your way. Christ, I wouldn't blame you for thinking your luck's never going to run out.'

'I'm really very attached to this pencil,' You-know-who said. 'Three important officers to return it – that's something. And the box! A most pleasant thought.'

'Who recruits your London triggers and knives for you? Are you still using Management Selection Inc.?' Iles inquired.

'What I've started to like as I grow a bit older, Mr Iles, is the quiet life,' You-know-who replied. 'And if all the decisions were left to me, that's how it would be. Of course, the brief wants me to go really hard at your lot and Mr Harpur personally about the prosecution and other matters. I expect your Chief has heard something about it already. What I mean, the brief would probably be able to make even a charming visit like this sound like harassment. You know what they're like, the Bar, every single one of them on the bones of their arses and not able to keep their cellars stocked with claret because of the truly pitiful fees they're allowed by the Government, and so they're always scraping for work, especially from people like me who can pay private. Mr Larnog is really pressing me to have a go. Myself, I try not to encourage him to think about making big trouble for you. After all, I knows you was only doing your job. He don't see things that way, though. Briefs like Mr Larnog are always looking for abuses by police, that sort of thing, persecution of targeted people, such as myself. He's very aggressive. Me, though, I'd like to curl up with a book about Clive of India and forget it all. Why can't we all just forget what's past, Mr Iles, Mr Harpur?'

Iles put his head on one side while seeming to give this consideration. He nodded a couple of times. 'That's certainly one way of looking at things, You-know-who.'

'What I mean, the system did find us not guilty, no matter how you messed about with the evidence.'

'Ah, yes, the dear old system.'

You-know-who stood up and paced a little near Iles's chair. For a second it looked as if he might put a friendly hand on the ACC's shoulder before he said what came next. He drew back from that but did bend over Iles and lowered his voice, making the words sound very intimate and heartfelt. 'Look, Mr Iles, I know there were special elements for you in this latest matter at Wood's house. Well, for one, you was knocking off the girl, Celia Mars, and I never heard anything but good said about her. So I can see you might take this very, very bad. That is a bloody terrible thing to have happened. It would go deep, I mean whoever done it.'

'Whoever done it, yes,' Iles replied.

'But, I mean, you still got a lovely wife, haven't you? Sarah, yes. Beautiful. And her and Mr Garland here have finished that thing between them, that's what I understand. So, it's not really so bad, is it? Most marriages need a bit of patching now and then. It's nothing to be ashamed of, Mr Iles.'

'Thank you,' Iles replied.

'And then there's this other stupid thing, I know, which might be putting the pressure on you, making you think you just got to clean everything up immediate in a way your boys will understand, the only way. Well, I don't really like to talk about it, but I heard about this poison going around among your lads in the Force. You know what I mean.'

Harpur watched Iles try to disguise his obvious bafflement and curiosity.

'These people saying you and Mr Harpur never really pushed the case against us because you was on the take – on my payroll. Keeping back some of the best evidence, that sort of thing.'

'Oh, that,' Iles said, smiling and nodding, as if he had heard it before.

'You know it's not true, Mr Iles, Mr Harpur, Mr Garland. I know it's not true. Maybe I wish it was true, but we won't talk about that. The thing is, though, that a lot of your lads do think it's true. That's what's doing the damage, isn't it?'

'It's certainly not pleasant,' Iles replied.

'So I'm hoping you won't let it bother you what they're spreading and turn you sort of mad nasty, especially that stuff they're saying about you meaning Street should get it in case he spilled about you being on the take. All that kind of rubbish will just blow away in a couple of months.'

'Of course it will,' Iles replied.

'We'll have to ask you to sign in duplicate for the return of the pencil,' Garland said.

'I think you ought to make Harpur put it back where he took it from,' Favard grunted.

In the car on the way to headquarters, Iles said: 'Had you heard these delightful rumours, Col?'

'About the supposed backhanders? No, sir.'

'Francis?'

'No, sir.'

'Do I understand the situation right, Col – he's been spreading this evil about us and is saying he'll go on doing it unless we take it easy on him?'

'That's how I read it, sir.'

'Francis?'

'Yes, I thought that was what we were being told, sir.'

'That I set Street up to be killed because we were Tom Suck-bribing from You-know-who and thought Street had found out from their end? Jesus Christ.' Iles was sitting alongside Harpur in the back and he cowered into the corner now, as if disabled by some gross shame. 'Our people can believe something like that?'

'I'm afraid it's possible, sir. You know police: they don't think the best of anyone, and especially not of police brass.'

'There's only one way to put a stop to thinking of that sort, isn't there?'

'Is there, sir?' Harpur replied.

'They've got an acquittal and one perfectly built alibi.'

'That's how it looks, sir.'

'So we forget about courts, about due processes,' Iles said. 'That's if we ever did think they could cope with this situation.' He brightened a little. 'I think I've got the layout of the house pretty clear in my head since this visit.'

'Yes, sir?'

'I believe I could find my way about in there, light or dark.'

'Yes, sir?'

'We can do without our surveillance unit there now, I think.'

'Yes, sir.'

15

They were dressing in the back of her Allegro, laughing and grunting as they struggled with their clothes, double-checking that nothing embarrassing was left on the floor or seat.

'By now we ought to be getting good at this,' Harpur said.

'I thought we were.'

'I mean the dressing in a shoe-box bit, hussy.'

'Oh, that. We do all right. I've never gone home wearing a pair of Y-fronts.'

He sat back and relaxed while Ruth wriggled for a while, getting her tights straight. It was a country-road lay-by they used now and then and shared with other steamed-up cars in the dark. In the mirror Harpur made out through the misted window the shape of a car backing up very close to the rear of the Allegro, much too close.

When Ruth was comfortable, she leaned against him, her face touching his. They had about fifteen minutes now for talking, and he enjoyed that. 'Anyway, don't rubbish car-love,' she said. 'It's a little world apart, isn't it, sealed in and separate – all that stuff about people cut off in their private bubbles on wheels. Well, that's OK. It's what suits us, a private bubble on wheels. Neither of us wants to go public, isn't that a fact, Col?'

'I suppose so. Not yet. How is it with you at home?'

'Oh, OK.'

'Yes, I'm OK, too, lately.'

'Except I've had to listen to a lot of abuse of you from Robert these last few weeks. I say nowt – just take it in and forget.'

'Yes?'

'Stupid stuff. Not about us, or anything like that.'

'To do with Ray Street?'

'You've heard?'

'That we deliberately put him where we knew he'd get killed for fear he'd muck up the trafficking and tell all about us. And then we didn't try to convict You-know-who and Favard because we're on the payroll. You know who's been planting the yarn?'

'Look, Col, I knew it was rot from start to finish, but I can't really answer back when Robert says it, can I? Why would I be defending you? Maybe he half-suspects you and me already: that little *faux pas* of mine at the wedding, and the rumours from far back, of course. So I try and let it all go over me. And that's why I like getting out with you in the little bubble now and then. It's slaggy, I know – just wed and here with an old boy-friend. Can't help it, though.'

Harpur was not paying much attention to what she said but watching the vehicle behind them with all the intentness of a peeping Tom.

'Robert's a damn good man, but he's one of the crowd, isn't

he? Most police are. He'll say what they say about you, think what they think. I don't blame him. They're trained to it. And he'd want to diminish you, wouldn't he? You could be right that You-know-who's been spreading it, but there was also some girl called Younger sounding off at a party in the Martyr after the acquittals. Someone on Robert's shift was sent to sort out the disturbance. This girl was apparently saying she should have been called at the You-know-who trial because she had special inside knowledge about Ray Street. But she never was. Her story was soon all around the shift and then all around the Force.'

Part of Harpur's brain still concentrated on the car behind them. Another part thought it detected from Ruth's tone that far, far back in her mind she wondered whether some of the rumour about himself and Iles was true.

He said: 'Iles has picked up these whispers, too. It's really knocked him. It knocks me, as well, but him worse. I don't know what he might do to put himself right?'

She turned and stared at him. 'You don't?'

'Perhaps I do. I'd have to clear up afterwards.'

'My God.'

'And I think I'd be glad to, if it stopped people believing muck like that about us.'

She gave a sudden little cry. 'What's this?' She did not seem to have noticed the car at the back, but now another drew in close ahead of them. They were boxed. The little bubble was not so private after all. Harpur sat up straight and was just about to get out to investigate when someone pulled the door open and three men in navy Balaclavas leaned in and grabbed him. There were a couple more behind them, also masked. He felt Ruth grip his arm and try to hold him in the car, like giving help to a drowning man, but these three knew what they were doing.

Two fixed on a shoulder and wrist each and the other took two handfuls of his jacket front and shirt. They all tugged together. He struggled and fought as hard as he could but his legs were trapped against the Allegro's front seat and he could not kick. Between them they could just about hold his arms.

They dragged him out, with Ruth still clinging to his jacket, and as soon as he was clear of the door the other two men took hold of him as well, and all five forced him down towards the ground. He had never been standing properly because he was crouched when he came out of the car, and they made sure he did not straighten, the five of them using their weight to push him flat. Together, they were strong, and he fell. Ruth's grip broke and for a second he saw her hanging half out of the Allegro, clutching for him.

One of them said: 'Stay clear, Mrs Cotton. This is for him, not you, though Christ knows what you're doing with him. Keep quiet. You wouldn't want to draw attention here, would you?'

The first of the kicks went into his balls, and as he tried to get his hands down there to protect himself he took another toe-cap on the wrist. For a while nobody said anything. They were hidden by the three cars from the rest of the vehicles, not that many of the couples would be looking out. Altogether, there were about a dozen kicks – thighs, kidneys, balls, knees. Ruth was sobbing, still part out of the car, part in. They stopped for a moment.

The man who had spoken earlier said: 'This is for Street and Peter Lowry, Harpur. What are you, recruiting office for the Halo Wall?'

He just about heard Ruth groan in amazement. 'You're police?'

'Someone's got to get the bastard, Mrs Cotton.'

Another voice said: 'And you're not going to say anything, are you, either of you? You don't want dear old Robert to know where you spend your Wednesday nights, do you? God, you're only a couple of months married.'

Thank Christ, they kept away from his head and face, so they were not aiming to mark him too badly, or kill him. He curled and did what he had been taught all those years ago, tried to neutralize the worst of it by making the body yield. But they knew about the training, too, and put the kicks in irregularly and unexpectedly, so he didn't always have time to counter.

'Your private income's not so bloody private, is it, Harpur?'

For a second, he thought about shouting a denial, if he could still shout, but what good would it do with this crew? They had been fed the lies and they had swallowed them whole.

When it ended, they piled swiftly into the two cars and left at once. For a while he lay waiting for the pain to ebb and trying to sort out whether any real damage had been done. One knee felt bad. He could taste no blood in his mouth, so nothing had started coming up from inside him yet. His wrist ached. Ruth leaned over and offered her hand to help pull him upright. 'Oh, love, oh, love,' she said. He still did not want to risk moving, in case he did himself deeper injury, and he waited another couple of minutes on the ground.

Then he carefully gripped her arm and got himself into a sitting position before trying to stand fully. 'We must change our routes and venues,' he said. Very slowly he straightened up. 'I'll go back to the office for a bit, maybe sleep there tonight. Hobbling about at home's not on.' He tried a step or two and it was bearable. After all, nobody wanted him to do a march past in Red Square.

A car door slammed and a man in his late fifties and a bit tousled walked towards them rather hesitantly. 'Look, I saw some of that and managed to get a registration number in my head. My car was dark and there was nowhere immediately available to write it down, but I think this is right: A098 LLP. In case you want to bring the police in, that is. Possibly not, I imagine. Would any of us? What were they, bloody muggers? A disgrace. Of course, they count on it not being reported because of the, well, confidential circumstances. It's dangerous here, but – well, I'll leave it to you to do whatever you wish. I'm afraid I can't offer to be a witness, but one couldn't let something like that go by without trying to help in some small measure. Do you think you might notify the police?'

'It's difficult,' Harpur replied.

'It is. Well, good night, both.' He strode to his Audi and climbed into the back.

'Motorized lovers of the world unite,' Harpur muttered.

The conversation had given him a little more time to recover and he did not feel quite so disabled now. Inspecting his clothes he found a big patch of blood coming through on the right thigh. With any luck it would not be spotted if he could get in quickly to his room at headquarters, and he'd try to pick a time for returning home tomorrow when Megan was shopping. Gently he eased himself into the Allegro and they drove away.

'Did you recognize any of them?' Ruth asked.

'Possibly. It hardly matters, though, does it? Am I going to do anything? They know I can't. Jesus, how they must hate me.'

'Darling, it's just mob malice founded on mob misinformation.'

'But I'm part of the mob, and they think I've let them down. Every day I agree a bit more with Iles: we've got to put ourselves right with the boys.'

'Sod the boys, I say. Thugs and idiots with everything wrong.'

'Most of it wrong.'

'Everything.'

'No, we've got two dead coppers. They're right on that. And we know who was behind it, and he's free. I'll get out here, love, and walk the rest. It will be a bit of therapy.'

'So, next week?'

'Of course. Why does it have to be so far off?'

16

Melanie Jill Younger parked her car in the street and then walked up You-know-who's long drive. It was a bright Sunday morning after heavy rain and she wore dark glasses against the glare, because she had woken up not feeling very good. Her sadness over Ray Street would not fade, and that surprised her. For maybe half a day when she first discovered he was a cop she had been so sick that she could hardly care about his death, and then this little spasm of resentment passed and it stopped mattering what his job had been. She felt she owed him something. All that counted was the fact they had been lovers – all that counted except he was dead.

The loss pain stayed with her and gave Jill very bad nights and mornings, and afternoons and evenings which were agonies, too. For relief she began snorting like a Hoover at a dandruff clinic, and this would usually do the trick for a time. The trick it did was to turn her grief into rage, the sort of rage against the killers of Street that had driven her to the Martyr after You-know-who's acquittal. This morning she had taken a cosy dose of coke to work that bit of magic, and she had felt the anger build wonderfully, like lust after a couple of gins. As a result, in her handbag now she carried a very high-quality kitchen knife, one of a set which she was normally afraid to use even in the kitchen, because they looked so grim. Perhaps she would be scared to use it here, as well, but just after she had helped herself to the boost this morning it had seemed a bonny idea to bring the knife on the visit. It still did.

She knocked on You-know-who's door.

The heavy snorting had cleaned out all her money weeks ago and she had drifted into whoring three or four nights a week. Twice before in her life she had taken money for it at bad times, and the fact that You-know-who had forced her back there now gave her hate and rage extra solidity. She wore the sun-glasses not just to keep out dazzle but to hide a split eye she had picked up the night before with a soldier client who wanted it free and turned very brutal when she said no.

Yes, it was a gorgeous life, thanks. Even with the tarting her cash did not keep pace with the new scale of her habit and she had borrowed a hundred pounds from her mother on the pretext that she wanted books and fees for an Open University course. 'Education is holy and the blood of the future,' her mother had said, handing over the twenties. It made Jill feel really grand to fleece her.

She knocked again on You-know-who's door, then opened her handbag and took hold of the knife handle.

On local television she had seen reports about the deaths of the airline man, a girl and another cop, and heard the commentator say there was a possible drugs-traffic link and point out that the airline man had given prosecution evidence in the Street trial. After that, she began to worry about her own safety. That scene at the Martyr must surely have put her on someone's list. A couple of times lately she had felt she was being followed. It was nobody she knew and, in fact, not always the same man. You-know-who would easily be able to hire for that kind of dirty job. Who the hell did they think they were, snooping and trying to terrorize her? She must look after herself, and that was another reason she had come today, with the knife. What was that line in the telly series? 'Do it to them before they can do it to you.'

She hammered on the door once more and then began to walk around the house, looking in at the windows. In the drive were two cars, so You-know-who and Favard ought to be here. She reached the rear of the house and a terribly neglected garden, with bits of stone statues and a sundial poking up through high grass and huge weeds. French windows looked on to this shambles and she approached these carefully, remembering from the time she watched the two of them return, that this was the part of the house they seemed to use. She sidled along the wall on the soaked soil, picking her way through brambles and weeds which grew right up to the house. Then, with her hand still on the knife, she looked around the edge of the open curtains.

She gave a short, high scream and pushed her mouth against the wall, to stop herself making any more noise. In her shock she found herself dribbling, and strings of her saliva swung from the rough cast, like that time she had spat at the television screen when the acquittals were announced. Then she looked again.

You-know-who lay on his stomach across the hearth rug, his head resting in the grate. Although no fire was alight there now, the side of his face visible to her was horribly burned, like pictures she had seen of accidents to wartime pilots. His hair was all gone and the skin of his scalp had puckered and parted in the heat. His shirt collar and the top of his jacket were scorched black. Cinders lay piled up near his face, as if they had been carefully arranged while still burning. One coal, as dead now as You-know-who, had been rammed into his mouth and was clamped by the exposed teeth and blackened lips.

Jill felt her lovely cocaine high drop from her like rain off a roof and her legs went feeble as she started to sweat. Again she pressed herself against the wall, but this time as a way to keep herself upright. Until the worst of the weakness went over, she put her handbag at her feet.

When she looked in again, she kept her eyes away from You-know-who and the fireplace. It was then that she saw Favard. He was facing the window, seated in a hard kitchen chair on the far side of the room, part in shadow. His feet were tied to the chair legs and it looked as if his hands were bound behind him. His eyes and his mouth were open, very and frighteningly open. She could make out a double strand of rope around his neck, cutting deep into the flesh, and behind his head what looked like a snapped-off section of a broom handle had been pushed under the ropes and used to twist and tighten them around Favard's neck. The piece of broom handle stood tight and straight against the back of his head, like a stiff plume on a helmet. In front of him, between the chair and the window, stood another kitchen chair with what looked from the back like a wall mirror propped on it, as if whoever had done that to Favard had wanted him to watch himself die. She started to think that someone who regarded vengeance as an art had been at work here. Did the painstaking way You-know-who had been placed so his face would burn mean something? There had been a fire at the airline man's house, hadn't there, and his body and the girl's burned beyond recognition? Was what had gone on here a reply to that?

She decided she ought to get away from Nightingale House fast. Her legs had recovered fairly well by now and she felt she would be able to reach the road. Bringing the kitchen knife seemed a comical waste of time in the circumstances, and she giggled for a second, but still took care not to look where You-know-who played a log. Could she have used the knife, had there been a chance? What did it matter? The sense of menace that had darkened things lately was suddenly gone. She felt sure that after this she would no longer fear someone was tailing her. She didn't have to do it to them before they did it to her because someone else had done it to them before she could try. She wished she knew who it was, so she could say thanks, from herself and from Ray Street.

She picked up her bag and made her way back around the house and then quickly down the drive to her car.

17

Lane was in his ancient office cardigan and had no shoes on as he paced the room, glancing out of the window occasionally towards the motor section and the town beyond. As always, he looked amiable and humane, though extremely tense. Iles, wearing a marvellous grey suit, watched the Chief tolerantly, a pad and pencil in front of him on the table, though he had written nothing yet. Suffering what he thought might be kidney pains after the kicking, Harpur was in an easy chair, and concentrated on finding a way to sit which caused him least distress.

Coming to a halt near Harpur's chair, the Chief said: 'I certainly don't want to exaggerate matters, but I feel we have a quite serious morale problem. All right, I've seen the same sort of thing in other Forces and, given a bit of time, it sorts itself out. Things go pretty deep here at present, though. It may sound a little pompous, but what we have on our hands appears to be a failure of confidence.'

'Confidence in what, sir?' Iles asked.

'In us – among the men.' Lane shuffled a few steps. Ever since Harpur had known him he had gone in for unkempt, relaxed styles: what Garland called 'the Chief's strident modesty.' Lane sighed. 'It really is grave. You've heard it all, I imagine – allegations of being on the take, conniving at the deaths of our own boys, and so on. We sink further and further into it, I'm afraid. Things were bad enough when we had only Street's death. Now there's Wood, Celia Mars, Lowry.'

'Well, we at least have people charged for those, sir,' Harpur said.

'We had people for Street,' Lane replied.

'We should be able to make things stick for the three taken at the reservoir, sir,' Harpur said.

'Unless the bloody jury believes them and decides it was the dead fellow who carried out the killings, against their wishes. Want to take bets?' Lane asked. 'In any case, these three are nobodies, aren't they, Colin? They're not the people we want. You-know-who and Favard carry on as ever. That's what our boys and girls see, and what they hate us for.'

Iles stirred a bit. 'When you say "us" you mean us, don't you, sir – Colin and me? You're reasonably well above it.'

'I mean the whole command structure. They see it as rotten, to the top.'

Iles said: 'Yes, it's sad, sir. We can't get any of our three prisoners to implicate You-know-who or Favard. They're nobodies, but they're pros. Or perhaps they genuinely don't know who was the paymaster. There could be middlemen. You-know-who would be bloody careful on a thing like this, however, lucky he may think he is. We've had our best interrogators on these three, Chat-up Charlie and Erogenous Jones, but nothing. So, we're going to look as if we're soft on You-know-who and Favard again.'

'They have an impeccable alibi for the time of the attack on Wood's house, sir,' Harpur said. 'We've been over it twenty different ways and it holds together.'

'Of course it does,' Lane replied. 'What does it really mean, though?'

'What it means is bugger all, sir,' Iles said, 'except in a court. They gave the orders and then made themselves safe. The point is, You-know-who has a genuine history of visiting his wife and kids regularly, and not just on access days. Neighbours tell us that. So, we can't argue that he made an exceptional effort to be out of town when Wood's place went up.'

165

Harpur added: 'Street went to the place once with him. It's a routine. He occasionally keeps some of his papers there, apparently. Like to see some of those, but we had no possible excuse for searching the ex-wife's house, or rather the ex-wife's husband's house.'

'A birthday party, wasn't it?' Lane asked.

'Yes, one of his kids was six. He gave him a sound-centre. A kid of six with a sound-centre?' Iles said. 'Col thinks it was originally bought for Street, as a peace offering after they'd failed to take him on the Dandy Lorraine outing.'

Lane folded himself into the chair behind his desk. 'Are we still keeping You-know-who and Favard under watch?'

'No, sir. There seemed no point,' Iles replied.

'So they do what the hell they like, in full view?'

Iles nodded sadly. 'I'm very much afraid that is so, sir. Colin and I simply don't know how to nail them. I have to admit they are able to make fools of us in any way they like.'

'Jesus,' the Chief said.

'This is one of those instances where patience is our main weapon, sir,' Iles advised. He picked up the pencil and wrote PATIENCE on his pad. 'It is a hard message to take, I know that, sir, especially for someone like you, so admirably sensitive to the feelings of our men and girls. We cannot, however, become a law unto ourselves. We only apply the law through a jury system which is still regarded as the greatest in the world, can you bloody believe it?'

'And you, Desmond,' Lane replied. 'In all the shit that's flying there's one story that says you and the messenger boy fink, Simon Wood, were knocking off Celia Mars in turn, and that your connections with the whole dirty outfit are . . . problematical. What's in it? Were you giving it to Mars?'

Iles rewrote PATIENCE on his pad carefully, before looking up to reply. 'We were lovers, yes, sir. She had become very important to me.'

'Well, my God, I mean, if You-know-who and his bloody lawyer proceed with complaints and we get an outside investigating officer to look at things and deal with the men's suspicions, what is he going to make of that?'

Iles said: 'One of the reasons I called off the surveillance at Nightingale House was that there would be less grounds for You-know-who to allege harassment.'

'That's all very well, Desmond, but – '

'Do you think then, sir, that my relationship with Celia implies I was on the take?' Iles asked.

'What? No, Christ, no. I never said that, or anything like that,' Lane replied, drawing the old cardigan around himself carefully, as if it were chain-mail.

Iles persisted. 'Were you, then, saying an officer from outside might infer that from the relationship?'

'Who knows what the bugger would infer? What he can see, let alone infer, is that two men known by everyone in the Force, if not the world, to be responsible for the deaths of two officers are sauntering about as if they'd bought us. Despite what you say, I don't understand why we haven't got a unit watching them. It would show we haven't given up, that we are a police force, not a gang of You-know-who's accomplices.'

'We can have the surveillance put back immediately, sir,' Harpur said.

'Certainly. I wouldn't object to that now,' Iles added.

'What does that mean – not object now?'

'Now you've pointed out that this is your wish, sir,' Iles replied. 'As to Celia Mars – '

'Look, Desmond, I don't want to poke into your private life.'

'That's touching, sir. I appreciate your consideration more than I can say. I feel I would like to explain, though. She knew nothing about Wood's sideline until I told her. She was a woman you would have found wholly pleasing, sir, embodying many of the characteristics you yourself prize and, if I may say so, reveal: humanity, good sense, loyalty, wit. As it happens, she hadn't gone to bed with Wood for more than two years, so it isn't true that he and I were – what was your word? – knocking her off in turn. Colin can bear me out as to this, can't you, Col?'

'Entirely.'

'One looked for a little solace and was fortunate enough to

find it in abundance,' Iles continued.

'All right, I accept all that,' Lane said. 'You have my sympathy. I mean, you're married to someone else and for me, as you know, that tends to rate as highly relevant, but I've seen the world.' He stood and shuffled around again. 'But all this leaves us still with the question of what to do about You-know-who and Favard.'

'There is absolutely nothing we can do, sir,' Iles replied sadly. 'Except listen to them giggle. Can we turn the fire against them as they did against others? I fear not, sir. There's a poem by the Frenchman de Vigny – '

'Oh, Christ, is there?' Lane said.

'It's called "The Death of the Wolf", and says all we can do is to get on with the job we've been given and not indulge stupid hopes. Always it's seemed to me a perfect gospel for police officers. We've lost on You-know-who, and we'd better face it.'

'I'm afraid I have to agree with that, sir,' Harpur added.

'Are you all right?' Lane asked.

'Sir?'

'You look like someone who's taken a hell of a skilled beating, no marks, but internal damage.'

Iles said: 'We've all taken a beating, sir. We'll come through.'

Harpur went back to the ACC's room with him. 'It's true, you are hobbling a bit, Col.'

'I fell, playing rounders with my daughters.'

'Man's lot is risk and pain.' He stared at his desk top. 'Oh, Lane is raw and brazen but I don't really dislike him for that. Does he know what love is, do you think? He's locked up for life with that cheerful old double-fronted wardrobe he married, so is he ever going to be able to understand passion, do you think? The Passion, yes, maybe, but a man and a woman outside marriage – that's "knocking someone off", isn't it, or "giving it to somebody"? You know, I pity him. Could he conceivably understand what a man might do if a woman he felt for was killed and burned by a wretch like You-know-who?'

'What might a man like that do, sir?'

168

Iles pondered this and then said: 'I'm genuinely fond of the Chief. Have you ever seen an adam's apple like his? He's done bloody well to get himself reasonably presentable when he's dressed up.'

'What might a man like that do, sir – the one whose girl was killed and burned?'

'As for me, I'm back to crossword puzzles with Sarah. They serve.'

'Good.'

'Of course, she's got something going. Don't know who. Not Garland now. I can't blame her for looking around.' He suddenly leaned across the desk towards Harpur. 'I miss Celia like hell.' His sharp features under the mass of grey hair had become full of sorrow.

'I understand.'

'So, I had to look for a little professional consolation. I know some sodding philosopher of your calibre is going to say it makes no sense to replace a woman one loved by a tart.'

'No, I wasn't thinking that, sir.'

'Ever been reduced to that, Col?'

'Paying for it?'

'She's got a little coke habit, I'd say. I'm helping fund it.'

'So the money might find its way to You-know-who.'

'I've considered that. Have to risk it, though. This girl's a little sweetie. *Petite.* Got a tattoo on her chest. She's read part of *The French Lieutenant's Woman.* As far as I can make out, she's had some big crisis in her life lately, though she doesn't say much. They never do, do they? She's not the golden-hearted whore we've all heard about, but she's got something.'

'Part of *The French Lieutenant's Woman*, sir?' Harpur said. Hadn't he heard something like that comical bit of faint praise before? He dredged his mind briefly before tracing the words to Ray Street. This was how Street had defended Melanie Jill Younger on the day Harpur had surprised the two of them in the tower-block flat. And other points seemed to fit: Iles thought the tart snorted, and it sounded as if she was slightly built. Also, Harpur recalled seeing the jaguar tattoo on her chest when he unwrapped her from the table-cloth. Was she on

the streets now, to help pay for her supplies, and had Iles somehow encountered her? It could easily happen. All the best girls
operated around the Valencia – Valencia Esplanade as it was
once grandly called, before urban rot set in. Jill would know
where to go, and the ACC would know where to look. If he was
searching for someone pretty and childlike – and his tastes had
been galloping towards nymphets before Celia temporarily
saved him – a meeting with Jill must always have been likely.
He would not recognize her. During the case he had refused
even to meet Jill, only read reports on what her evidence might
have been. And Harpur could not remember any pictures of
her. 'Has your girl got a name, sir?'

'Think you know her? How?'

'No. Only general interest.'

'Just keep off. I'm not sure how many men I share her with
already, but it's enough. I know her phone number, and the
four nights she works. It's something. No, it's everything.'

'And why not, sir?'

'So kind, you patronizing bastard.'

18

During her brief return to the game Melanie Jill Younger had
acquired two regular clients among all the rest. One was a post-
man in his forties, a widower with insurance money to spend
since his wife's death. The other she could not really sort out.
Grey-haired but youthful, he was gentle and sometimes very
funny, and he always paid over the odds. His clothes were
good and he had what her father used to call an officers'-mess
accent. He didn't say much, nothing like as much as the post-
man, but she had the idea he was bright and saw much more
than he seemed to. In some ways he made her unsettled, but
she could not decide why. There was something sad and something a bit cracked about him, but as punters went he had to be
in the top bracket.

Tonight, when he was sorting out the cash for her after-wards, he said: 'Little girl, you don't seem too well to me. And who cut your eye?'

'Wasn't it any good? You want to take a fiver off?'

'Not that. It was fine, love. But you seem – well, I don't know, you seem to be in shock. And it's not just the cocaine.'

'What are you talking about?' she muttered. 'What cocaine?' Jesus, yet another cop? Why hadn't she thought of that when trying to place him? Wasn't he too well-dressed for a cop, though?

'Well, as long as you're all right.'

'You can't do that. What coke are you talking about?'

'OK, let's forget about coke. There isn't any. I made a mistake.'

'Look, I don't want no bother.'

'What bother?'

'I know a lot about bother. I've had enough for a long, long time.'

'That's what's upsetting you, is it? You don't have to worry because of me.'

'How come you picked me?' She sat up in the bed, small, thin and tense.

'You're very pretty.'

'Yes? Is that all?'

'What else?'

'You wasn't looking for me, I mean, looking for me special?'

'I was looking for someone as pretty as you, special.'

'Sometimes you really scare me.'

'How come?' He had finished counting the money and handed it to her.

'You police?'

'Police? Why do you say that?'

'They gets everywhere.'

'Yes, I suppose so. But I must be off now. Perhaps Tues-day?'

'Listen, if you're police and you're spying on – '

'Calm down, love. I'm away now.'

'You know I'm tied up in something big, do you? There's

going to be trouble for me?'

'I don't know what you're – '

'Listen, you promise me there'll be no trouble, and I can tell you something really big. As a matter of fact, I've been wanting to tell someone. It's getting me down.'

He came back and sat on the bed. 'You're in a real fret.'

'This is something terrible, but none of it is my fault. You got to believe me.'

'Terrible?' He had a laugh about that, as if she could not possibly know anything important. 'Go on then, if you want to get it off your chest.'

She hesitated for a second. Why tell this stranger, cop or not? It might bring bother, no matter what he promised. That's how police lived, by bringing bother. They got fat on it.

But then the thought of still sitting on this secret alone hit her and she crumpled. 'Listen, I found two bodies.'

'Yes?'

'They'd been done in and one had a bit of coal shoved into his mouth.'

'Coal? Why so?'

'How the hell do I know? I only found them, that's what I'm telling you. Don't you bloody care about this? You sound like you knew it already, you know that?'

'It does seem big, as you say.'

'And these people, the deads, they're not nobodies. These are some of the biggest villains you ever heard of, called You-know-who and Favard.'

'Yes? I think I've heard of them.'

'So, listen, if I tell it all, give you the address and everything, you can leave me out of it, right? You'll get promotion for this, won't you?'

'It's no use to me, love. I'm not in that business. If I were you, what I'd do is dial 999.'

'I thought, like, we could do a deal.'

'Just dial 999 and tell them. You don't have to mention who you are. Say it and ring off.'

'It was like someone real mad or very, very angry had been to that house and done it.'

'Oh, angry, I'd say, not mad. Not mad at all.'

'One of the bodies had been pulled to the fireplace so the head would be right in the grate.'

'I'd really dial 999. Keep your name right out of it. They'll want to know how you're involved, otherwise. You know what bloody police are.'

19

Harpur was at home being given some instructions by his younger daughter on how to play a guitar when the Control Room telephoned to say that You-know-who and Favard had been found dead.

'Christ, we've got surveillance on that house,' he replied.

'It must have happened while the watch was lifted, sir. They've been dead a while.'

'Does Mr Iles know about this?' Harpur re-cast the question: 'Have you informed him?'

'Oh, yes, sir. He's going to the house, I believe.'

'How did we find out?'

'Anon 999. A woman or girl.'

'Saying?'

'Two corpses, one with a coal in its mouth, at Nightingale House.'

'With what?'

'Yes, sir, a coal. There's a sort of fire motif. In a way it's appropriate – tidies things up very nicely. That's the general view, sir.'

'What does that mean, for God's sake?'

'That's the general view, sir. A bit of a party has broken out in the bar.'

When Harpur arrived at the house Garland was already there. 'A couple of things, sir. Sergeant Fray, the Fingers, tickled the combination safe and we've got You-know-who's papers showing plenty about the coke deals and routes.'

You-know-who must have brought them back from his ex-wife's place, which was considerate of him.

Garland continued. 'It looks as if someone stood outside near the french windows, a woman in heels. A small woman. Could be the informant. You-know-who was shot in the chest before being burned. Favard was garrotted.'

'Yes, I can see. He was never pretty, mind.'

'All the boys here are pretty pleased, sir. It's as if a real load has been lifted.'

Harpur put a handkerchief over his nose. 'I'd say they've been dead at least a week.'

'Oh, at least. It's going to be virtually impossible to pick up leads, wouldn't you say?' He sounded very hopeful.

'Yes, impossible,' Harpur replied.

Lane and Iles arrived together. 'This is appalling,' Lane said. 'How the hell is it going to look from outside?'

'Simply like an extension of gang war, sir,' Iles replied.

'We're here to stop that, damn it,' the Chief said.

'Errors are bound to get through, sir.'

'I don't like it,' Lane said.

'On the other hand, I do, sir,' Iles told him.

'I'll never understand why surveillance was lifted on the house long enough for these terrible things to happen.'

'It seemed reasonable at the time, sir,' Iles said.

Later that night Harpur was seeing Ruth. They had abandoned their lay-by after the attack and driven out to a forest road and parked. Just after they had moved into the back and were undressed the door was pulled open and Harpur saw several men in Balaclavas. 'Oh, Christ,' he said.

'No, it's OK, Mr Harpur. We came to say thanks. You got the message good, the one we left last time.'

'Thanks?'

'The way things have gone.'

'Not me.' Once before in his career he had been credited like this: praised for an illegal cleansing operation he had not carried out.

'No, we know you didn't do it, sir. But you could pass the congratulations on, couldn't you? On and up? We thought that was the best way. Could you manage that for us? We don't want to hang about. You two must be getting cold. Can you deal with that, then, sir?'

'I think so.'

'Great. We'll leave you to it. No leads on the Nightingale killings yet, we understand?'

'Hopeless.'

'Great. You can keep it like that?'

'Well, the Chief's very keen we should catch whoever – '

'Up the Chief.' They slammed the door shut.

Ruth said: 'Friends of yours?'